The Secret of the East Wind

CAROL GIFT PAGE/DORIS ELAINE FELL

HARVEST HOUSE PUBLISHERS
Eugene, Oregon 97402

All persons and groups of persons named in this book are fictional; any resemblance to actual persons or groups of persons is purely coincidental.

SECRET OF THE EAST WIND

Copyright © 1986 by Carole Gift Page and
  Doris Elaine Fell
Published by Harvest House Publishers
Eugene, Oregon 97402

ISBN 0-89081-514-3

Printed in the United States of America.

To Jeff and Saundra Geston
who have their own beautiful love story
and to
the more than 58,000 men and women
whose names are inscribed
on the Vietnam Veterans Memorial Wall
in Washington, D. C.

The Secret of the East Wind

CHAPTER ONE

Dreaming.

A faceless man looms up from the shadows, his hands stretching through the swirling mist, groping, urgent. My heart pounds. I know this man—he is both familiar and terrifying—yet I cannot quite recognize him. Who is he to strike such panic within me?

I try to run. I am breathless with running. But I cannot move. Cannot escape. My limbs are numb, paralyzed. I try to scream but have no voice. I am detached from my body. I watch in wordless horror as the faceless intruder towers over me. At his touch, my frame collapses, disintegrates like parchment devoured by flames.

I awake, sit bolt upright in bed, trembling, my palms icy, my spine throbbing with tension. The nightmare clings like a milky web, refusing to be shaken. I rise and roam my small apartment, flicking on all the lights, turning on the radio and TV, peering around every dark corner and crevice.

I try to pray, but my mind is fragmented, my thoughts scattered like dry leaves in an autumn wind. I summon only one compelling prayer: I want David!

I sit on the sofa and hug my arms around me, pretending they are David's arms. I close my eyes and imagine his kiss until my nocturnal terrors abate.

● ● ●

At last, with the first pale rays of dawn, I went to my kitchen and plugged in the coffee pot. A hot cup of coffee would take away the chill of this crisp November morning and keep me awake after a sleepless night. I even relented and helped myself to a gooey jelly doughnut, but it felt dry and tasteless, and it caught in my throat.

The only good thing about this Monday morning was that I would be seeing David at work—David Ballard, owner of the progressive and profitable Ballard Computer Design Corporation. Three weeks ago he was only my handsome, elusive boss. Now, after our harrowing Morro Bay adventure—pitting us against a ruthless cocaine syndicate—and last Friday evening's romantic interlude in Laguna Beach, we were on the verge of making a permanent commitment.

As I sipped my coffee, I relived our Friday evening together as I'd done a thousand times this weekend ...David's tender kisses and whispered promises, a candlelit table for two silhouetted against a flaming sunset, David and I strolling arm-in-arm over the wet, packed sand through a twilight paradise of boulder-strewn cliffs and a sapphire sea...

I dreamily poured a second cup of coffee, then glanced in alarm at the clock. Seven o'clock already! With reluctance I put away my pastel dreams of David and hurried to the bedroom. I slipped into my beige designer suit and silk, rust-toned blouse, brushed my long, tawny hair until it glistened, then, with a toss of my head, strode out to my little brown Honda and caught the freeway north to Irvine.

The moment I entered the lobby at work, I was met by sly glances and curious stares. It had been this way ever since David and I had returned from Morro Bay two weeks ago. In a way, we had become instant heroes—unwittingly cracking open one of the largest cocaine syndicates on the West Coast. What had started out as a simple business trip in David's private plane had nearly cost us our lives, but during those incredible, terrifying days, we had managed to fall deeply in love.

As I approached my desk, Eva Thornton, David's longtime friend and administrative assistant, greeted me like a protective mother hen and warned, "The office is buzzing with rumor and innuendo, Michelle."

"What's up?" I asked, puzzled.

"David arrived this morning with a model of a fancy sailing ship."

"A model ship—brass and handcrafted?"

"Uh-hmm," said Eva with a wink. "With *Michelle's El Morro* engraved on the bow."

My face felt warm. "We—David bought that in Morro Bay."

"I know. And I suspect that was David's way of making his own little announcement. He strode in here this morning as businesslike as you please, with that ship tucked under his arm. But he made it a point to stop at a desk or two so that the secretaries could admire his treasure."

"He was that obvious?" I felt good inside, pleased. "Did Mitzi see it?" I inquired slyly.

Eva laughed aloud. "Mitzi Piltz is the one who got the rumors flying. You know how she is with the office scuttlebutt."

"I know, and she's had her eye on David since she came to work here."

"And her third divorce isn't even cold yet," said Eva, glancing around covertly. She touched my hand. "Come to my office, Michelle, or you'll be besieged with questions from the secretarial pool. Mitzi has them convinced that you've won the heart of David Ballard, and they're all intensely jealous!"

In the privacy of Eva's luxurious suite, she bombarded me with questions of her own. "I've got to know, Michelle. David's not saying a word, and I've been his confidante for years. In fact, I've been trying to get you two together since you came to work here six months ago. It's time David settled down." She stopped, breathless, waiting.

"What do you want to know?" I laughed.

With her tapered, polished fingers, Eva patted a wisp of gray-blonde hair into place and pursed her plum-red lips. "Everything! From the beginning!" Her dark brown eyes snapped with excitement.

"Well, the cocaine syndicate that my friend Jackie's husband was involved in—"

"No, not that, not that. You and David have already told me about your Morro Bay adventure. I want to know what happened between you and David at Laguna Beach."

I felt the color rise in my cheeks. "Nothing happened," I protested.

"Oh, I know that. David is an honorable man, as self-disciplined as they come." She leaned over confidentially. "But tell me the truth, he must be terribly romantic, too!"

Now I really blushed! "I don't know what to tell you. We—we love each other."

"Go on, go on," Eva urged.

There was something in Eva's warm, caring manner that made her questions seem more like loving concern than intrusive prying. I knew she loved David like a son.

"David is wonderful," I confided. "In Morro Bay he turned my life around completely. But we haven't made any definite plans. In fact, until this past weekend I'd hardly seen him since we got back from Morro Bay."

"Two weeks of silence? Isn't that just like David! But, of course, you realize he was all wrapped up in the pile of work on his desk."

"I know that's all it was," I murmured. "But I must confess I was growing pretty anxious. For a couple of weeks I was embarrassed about coming to work. I kept thinking, if David really loved me, why didn't he call?" I was silent a moment. Even now I didn't feel quite free to share with Eva the little, lingering fear that David's tenderly proclaimed love might be, in reality, merely kindness or sympathy. After all, he had talked about a permanent commitment, but he hadn't mentioned marriage. With his powerful, independent nature and his workaholic habits, would he ever need—or have time for—a wife?

Eva must have sensed my sudden reticence. "Am I meddling too much, Michelle? If I am, just tell me to mind my own business."

I patted her hand reassuringly. "Oh, Eva, you

could never be meddlesome. You've been a dear friend since I came to Southern California. Who else do I have to confide in?"

"The good Lord," smiled Eva with another wink.

I nodded emphatically. "You're right, Eva. I'm convinced if it hadn't been for the Lord, David and I never would have made it home from Morro Bay alive."

As I stood up to leave, Eva gave me a probing glance. "Before you go to your desk, Michelle—"

"Yes, Eva?"

"Maybe I shouldn't say this—"

"What is it?"

"For a gal who's just had a wonderful weekend, you don't look very rested. I hope it's not your concern over David's intentions. He's a man of his word—"

"I'm sure he is, Eva. Don't worry. I'm not lying awake at night just thinking about David. It's something else—"

"What, Michelle?"

I sat back down and shook my head slowly. "To tell you the truth, what little sleep I've managed is plagued by nightmares."

"Nightmares? About David?"

"No—of our entire Morro Bay experience. I keep envisioning the faces of my captors. Sometimes they're faceless, and that's even worse. I find myself running, stumbling, picking myself up, breathless with terror, the entire drug syndicate pursuing me with a fiendish glee. The moment one of them catches me, I wake up in a cold sweat, screaming."

Eva's face blanched. "Does David know?"

"I haven't told him. I wouldn't want him to know I'm being such a ninny."

"You're not, Michelle," Eva said fervently. Her mouth twitched slightly. "I know from experience that fears and nightmares can be devastating."

I looked at Eva in surprise. "You're always so confident, so in control. I can't imagine you ever being afraid."

Eva's gaze lowered. She fingered the band of her jeweled watch. "There was a time in the past when nightmares almost destroyed my sanity."

"Oh, Eva, that's just how I feel sometimes. Tell me, how did you get over them?"

"It was a long, painful journey. I was lost, floundering. Then, thanks to David, I met the Good Shepherd. Even then, learning to trust Him was a slow, groping process until finally the hellish dreams were gone."

"I guess that's one reason I haven't told David about my dreams," I confessed. "I feel my faith—that God should—"

Eva smiled supportively. "It doesn't always work that way."

"Your nightmares—did you know what caused them?"

Eva was silent for a minute. There was a wistful, faraway look in her eyes. "Perhaps you don't know, Michelle. I had a son—" Her voice quivered slightly.

"I didn't know, until recently—"

Eva smiled through misty eyes. "Rob was my whole life, my only child."

"David told me about Rob—what good friends they were—"

"Yes. Best of friends. They served together in Vietnam."

"David said he was with Rob when he died."

"That's right. Rob died shortly after their Navy

Phantom crash-landed during a reconnaissance mission." She gazed off into space. "For as long as I live, I'll never forget the day they told me my son was dead."

"I'm so sorry, Eva." The pain etched in her face was as fresh as if she'd just heard the news. I wanted to reach out and touch her, but she sat with such stoic pride that I was afraid to intrude on her emotions.

"And then the nightmares started," she continued. "For weeks after Rob's death, I cried myself to sleep. I'd dream of the plane crashing, grenades exploding, my son lying there broken, faceless, alone."

"Oh, Eva! Was it always the same dream?"

She nodded. "Always."

"How long did the dreams go on?"

"For months—until David came back to the States. He kept his promise to Rob and looked me up. He took hold of my hand and told me how much my son loved me."

"And that's how you and David became friends?"

Eva smiled, remembering. "We practically became mother and son. I guess we needed each other. David's parents were dead. I was a widow. David was like Rob in so many ways—full of lofty dreams and goals. But David had found faith while in Vietnam—a faith in Christ he shared later with me." She choked with emotion as she added, "I only wish I could have shared Christ with my son."

"Maybe someone else did," I offered.

She smiled wanly. "I only wish I knew. But it's too late. I'll never know."

Softly I said, "I'm beginning to understand why you and David needed each other."

"Yes, David really filled a void in my life. He

showed me how to have fun again. He taught me to play tennis and chess. I taught him to appreciate classical music and light opera. After his Navy discharge we pooled our expenses and moved to California. I lent him the money I received from Rob's life insurance policy to start his computer company, and David took me on as his right hand assistant. With David's ingenuity and the Lord's blessing, the business has just mushroomed."

"And you said eventually the nightmares stopped?"

"Yes, they stopped. Now I dream of Rob only once in a while—mostly happy, pleasant memories."

"Oh, Eva, my nightmares seem so insignificant compared to yours."

"Not really, Michelle. Fear is gripping, overpowering. It takes time to forget painful memories and to eventually see God's hand in one's life."

"I'm learning slowly," I confessed.

Eva picked up her pen and tore the top sheet from her notepad. "Here's my home phone number, Michelle," she said, writing quickly. "The next time you have a restless night—a frightening dream—call me. It doesn't matter what hour."

I tucked her phone number in my suit pocket. "I've got to run, Eva," I said. "In love with the boss or not, I've still got to do an honest day's work."

Eva smiled fondly. "He'll love that about you, too."

CHAPTER TWO

It was after 8:30 A.M. when I left Eva's office and sat down at my own desk in the central office. As I slipped a sheet of paper into my typewriter, I looked up and saw David making his way toward me. He was a tall, athletic man, suntanned and immaculate in his three-piece brown suit with oyster-white shirt and conservative tie. He caught my eye and broke into a generous grin, his deepset eyes crinkling merrily.

I smiled briefly, then gazed back at my work, not wanting my colleagues, or even David, to catch the stars in my eyes. Something leaped inside me every time I saw him—his strong jaw and perfectly carved features, his shock of chestnut hair, and the mischievous twinkle in his mahogany eyes. The only thing that marred his strikingly handsome face was the jagged scar tracing the cleft of his chin—an eternal reminder of the grenade explosion in Vietnam that had claimed Rob Thornton's life.

From the corner of my eye I saw David give a

quick nod to Mitzi Piltz, the gossipy secretary across from me—a thirtyish strawberry blonde, dressed to kill, whose shrewd green eyes never missed a thing. "Good morning, Mr. Ballard," she crooned pleasantly, fluttering her mascara-thick lashes.

"Good morning, Mitzi," David replied. Glancing at me, he added, "Have you ever seen a more beautiful day?"

"Oh, never!" Mitzi gushed, flicking a perfumed hanky. "Why, I was just telling my ex—"

"And how are you today, Michelle?" I felt my cheeks grow warm as David ambled around my desk, bent down, and blew a kiss in my ear.

"Not here, David," I whispered, looking furtively at Mitzi. "People will talk."

"Let them. It's all true, Michelle. I don't care who knows. The boss is crazy about one of his employees."

"You're being impetuous," I scolded as he squeezed my hand. Feeling Mitzi's eyes on me, I said with mock formality, "How can I help you, Mr. Ballard?"

His well-modulated voice lowered. "By quitting and marrying me today."

I felt my face flush a deep crimson. "I thought I had to give a two-week notice."

He winked. "In extreme cases, I bypass that requirement."

I stole a glance at Mitzi. She was watching raptly, her darkly penciled brows arched in astonishment.

"I can't marry you today, David," I said, playing along. "We don't have a license."

"We could fly to Vegas."

Mitzi gasped.

"In your private plane?" I teased.

"Are you kidding?—After what happened the first

time?—After my Bonanza crash-landed us smack in the middle of that hornets' nest of cocaine traffickers?" He heaved a mocking sigh and said, "We'll play it safe and go commercial."

My phone rang and startled us both. "Miss Merrill," I answered brightly into the mouthpiece. "Oh, Eva. Yes, David's here." I extended the phone to him. "It's Eva."

"Yes, Eva? What's up?" He frowned slightly. "Blair Publishers?—Can you handle it?" He gave me a disappointed grimace. "Okay, I'll call them right back, Eva." He twirled the receiver and dropped it into its cradle. "Business," he announced.

"Then you're too busy to marry me today?" I quipped.

He nodded.

"So the wedding's off?"

"Not for long," he assured me.

I glanced at my left hand, the ringless finger. Was David serious? Did he really want to marry me? He said he loved me but there had been no talk of a ring, no real proposal until now. But was this flirtatious banter a serious proposal?

David ran his fingertips gently over my arm. "There will be a wedding," he said, more seriously, "with a diamond ring and all the trimmings. But first I need an address."

"An address? The jeweler's?"

"No. Your parents."

"My parents? Whatever for? Are you going to Illinois to visit them?"

"No, Eva's going to type a letter for me."

"To my parents? Have I done something wrong?"

David's eyes glistened with that irresistible twinkle of his. "If you call making your boss fall in love with you wrong."

"Then why the letter, David?"

"I'm old-fashioned. I want to ask permission to marry their daughter."

My heart skipped a beat, several beats. I caught a glimpse of Mitzi, her mouth gaping, fanning herself nervously. Gazing back at David, I said with feeling, "Why don't you ask the daughter first?"

"I thought I did, a few minutes ago."

"I wasn't sure you were serious."

"I'm always serious where you're concerned." He straightened. "May I have the address, Michelle?"

As I jotted it down, David strolled over to Mitzi and put a comradely hand on her shoulder. "You know, Mitzi," he said confidentially, "I'd just as soon this conversation be kept among the three of us."

Mitzi waved her long, ruby-red nails in a gesture of suppressed agitation. "Oh, Mr. Ballard, you know you can depend on me." She pretended to zip her lips. "They're forever sealed, I swear it."

I smiled privately and mused under my breath, "Sealed—until the first coffee break!"

David tucked my parents' address into his vest pocket, turned, and strode toward his office. While he was still within hearing distance, I called, "Mr. Ballard, Eva doesn't have to write your letter. '*Speak for yourself, John.*' "

He pivoted and grinned. "Good idea! What's that from—Shakespeare?"

"No. Longfellow. *The Courtship of Miles Standish.*"

"I thought Shakespeare was your bag."

"He is. But Longfellow comes in handy once in awhile, too."

"Tell you what. Meet me in my office in an hour with your parents' phone number. We'll call them on the conference phone."

"Then you're really serious?"

"Never more...quoth the raven."

"Poe!" I said.

"Poe, with a little of David Ballard thrown in."

We both laughed. Inside, my heart was doing somersaults, stealing my breath completely. It was incredible. The cool, dignified, no-nonsense David Ballard had just proposed marriage before all of heaven and earth and the unflappable Mitzi Piltz.

Exactly one hour later I stood outside David's office, knocking lightly on his carved mahogany door. I knew he liked promptness.

"Come in, Michelle."

I entered just as he swiveled around in his leather chair.

"You're certainly sure of yourself," I teased.

"I was certain it was you. You're right on time." He stood and with a gallant, sweeping gesture indicated the chair across from his massive desk.

As I sat down, David pressed the intercom button and said, "Hold my calls, Mitzi. If there's anything major, have Mrs. Thornton take it." Then he looked back at me and said with confidence, "Well, Michelle, let's call your folks and get their blessing on our marriage plans."

"Maybe you'd better call Dad's pharmacy. He'll be at work now." I slipped a number across the desk to him.

He arched one brow quizzically. "Andrew's Apothecary?"

I nodded.

With a quick hand, David punched the appropriate digits. Then, placing the phone on "conference call," he winked reassuringly at me.

As we waited, I glanced around nervously. Like David, his office was orderly and masculine. Everything he needed was here, everything in its place—his personal computer and printer, calculator, and high-speed telephone modem. It was obvious that he had rearranged the items on his desk to make room for the polished, handcrafted sailing ship, its brass trimmings accenting the browns and earth tones of his office.

Behind him, within arm's reach, was a ready reference library—books on stock investments, computers, tennis, and American history that so intrigued him. His Bible was there on the shelf too, worn with use, along with antique editions of Melville and Poe. How David found time for pleasure reading, I didn't know. But since reading, tennis, and flying were his favorite forms of relaxation, he managed somehow to work them into his busy schedule.

Finally, after several rings, Dad's voice boomed into the room. "Andrew's Apothecary. Andrew Merrill speaking."

"Mr. Merrill, this is David Ballard."

"Yes?"

"I'm David Ballard," David repeated with emphasis.

"You said that already," Dad responded impatiently.

David squirmed. "Yes, sir. I'm calling about your daughter."

"Which one?"

"Michelle. The pretty one," David added, trying for lightness.

"They're both pretty." Then more urgently, "Is Michelle all right?"

"Sir, she's fine. We're—" David plunged in. "Mr. Merrill, your daughter and I want to get married."

"You what?" he exploded.

"Mr. Merrill, I'm calling to ask for your permission."

"You're telling me you want to get married, Mr.—?"

"Ballard," David offered.

I should have warned David. I had forgotten how obstinate and exasperating Father could be.

"Where are you calling from, young man?"

"Irvine, California, sir."

"Could you be more specific?"

David scowled. He wasn't accustomed to being interrogated. His jaw clenched with determination, accenting the scar on his chin. "Ballard Computer Design in Irvine—the office where Michelle works."

"Is my daughter there?"

"I'm here, Father," I said meekly. "With David."

"Are you all right?"

"Of course. I'm fine."

"And you want to get married?" There was a raspy squeak to Father's voice. "Just like that. You never even mentioned this man to me—and you're talking marriage?"

"Dad, I did mention him—in the letter I wrote two weeks ago about Morro Bay. Honestly, Dad, David is wonderful. He's a Christian. We're—"

For a moment Dad weakened. "A Christian, you say? You're sure?" Then the battle resumed. "Isn't this a little premature? You haven't even had time to get over Scott."

I resented the mention of my first love—my college sweetheart, Scott, who had broken our engagement to elope with one of my closest girlhood friends. My parents had been openly opposed to Scott, who vocally challenged their traditional Christian values. "I'll always remember Scott," I said softly. "But I'm in love with David."

"So where did you meet this young man?" demanded Dad.

"I told you in the letter—on a plane ride—we were together in Morro Bay—"

David quickly countered with, "Actually we met several months ago when Michelle came to work here."

That did sound better. We could hear Dad suck in his breath; the sound vibrated through the microphone.

"Sir," David began again, "we called to ask your permission to marry. I love your daughter very much. I can provide for her. We believe the Lord—"

We could hear the door bang at Andrew's Apothecary, then Father's muffled voice saying, "Yes, your prescription's ready, Mrs. Rafferty...I'll be with you in a minute...my daughter Michelle's calling long distance..."

Then he was back. "Michelle?" He sounded old now, defeated. "California's so far away."

I winced inwardly. "I know, Daddy, but we'll visit often." Privately, I wondered, Was Dad still holding onto his lifelong dream of having me come home and take over the family business when he retired? Or was he thinking of my near-mistake with Scott? I waited with growing apprehension.

"Could I have your number there at work, Michelle? I need to go home and talk to your mother, tell her what's happening."

"When will you call back, Mr. Merrill?" David interjected.

"Within the hour," Dad said wearily.

"Let me give you the company's toll-free number," said David.

Dad would like that.

There was an uncanny silence in David's office after Dad hung up. I was angry and embarrassed over my Dad's rudeness. David came slowly around the desk and took both my hands in his. He leaned down and kissed me gently. "Maybe we should have flown to Vegas."

"I should have let Eva write your letter," I acknowledged.

We laughed half-heartedly.

Finally I sputtered, "It's not like I'm some infatuated teenager. I'm twenty-four years old."

David was solemn. "Maybe your parents won't want you marrying an older man."

I emitted a spontaneous chuckle. "Oh, David, really! I don't consider a man in his thirties *old!*" I crinkled my nose at him. "Besides, there's ten years difference between my mother and dad."

David looked encouraged. "Then there's hope for us."

"Listen, David," I said seriously, "I don't need Dad's permission to marry."

David embraced me tenderly and murmured, "Maybe I'm just old-fashioned, Michelle. But if the Lord really wants us together—and I believe He does—He's going to give us your parents' blessing."

I wasn't entirely convinced of David's logic, but I loved him even more for the high-principled strength he was offering me now.

"Are you sure your dad will call back?" he asked.

"Oh, yes. He keeps his word. If I know Dad, he's already put the "CLOSED" sign in the window and is hurrying home to Mother. The house is just two blocks from the drugstore. He'll lumber, panting into the kitchen, and Mother will be certain he's having a heart attack."

"He has heart trouble?"

"Every time his daughters want to do something he doesn't approve of. Even when I left for California, he reminded me that he still expected me to take over the drugstore someday."

"But you're not a pharmacist."

"I know. My younger sister Pam came the closest. She just got her degree in nursing. She keeps promising to come visit me soon."

David was about to respond when Dad's call came through. "Mr. Ballard," Mitzi apologized in her honey-toned voice, "there's a long distance call for you—a Mr. Merrill from Lake Forest, Illinois. The man insists on speaking to the president of the company. I tried to get him to talk to Mrs. Thornton..."

"It's okay, Mitzi. I'll take the call in here." David clasped my hand and pressed the receiving button. "Mr. Merrill?"

"I want to speak to the president." Dad was in control now, his tone commanding.

"Speaking," David told him. "How can I help you, Mr. Merrill?"

"I'm calling to inquire about one of your employees, a Mr. David Ballard. He's asking to marry my daughter. I'd like to know what sort of fellow he is. Can you vouch for him?"

"Uh, Mr. Merrill, I can assure you Mr. Ballard's intentions are honorable."

"You know him that well?"

"Yes, sir. You see, I am Mr. Ballard. I own and

operate the company. I'm the one who wants to marry your daughter."

There was a moment of silence as Dad digested this stunning bit of news. But he was not rebuffed. "Well, Mr. Ballard, if that's who you are, Michelle's mother is here with me. We've been talking—"

"Michelle, dear, are you there?" Mother interrupted.

"Yes. Did Dad tell you our news?"

"He tried. I asked him if it's the young man from Morro Bay."

"Yes," I said eagerly. "You'll love David, Mother!"

"What matters is whether you do."

"Very much."

"Michelle, you've always wanted a garden wedding." Mother hesitated. I could hear the wistfulness in her voice. "But the weather is too cold now, dear. The garden won't be in bloom until springtime . . ."

"What Mother means," Dad interrupted, quickly dampening our spirits, "is that it hasn't even been a year since Scott. Maybe the excitement of all you went through with Mr. Ballard in Morro Bay is putting stars in your eyes." He cleared his throat. "Maybe it's rebound, Michelle—a chance to get even with Scott—"

David stiffened. "Mr. Merrill, it seems that the only person having difficulty forgetting Scott is you."

I put a restraining hand on David's shoulder. Things were not going well. "Get through to Mother," I mouthed.

"Mrs. Merrill—Mr. Merrill. I want to marry your daughter. We're hoping for your blessing."

"Daddy," Mother coaxed, "it's a straightforward request. Aren't you going to answer Mr. Ballard?"

There was a pause. We could hear Mother's muffled words. Scolding? Persuading? Disagreeing? We couldn't tell. "Mother, we—we wouldn't have called," I stammered, "if we thought it would be such a problem."

"We won't stand in your way," she answered stoutly.

Dad's tone was mellow now. "I respect you for calling, Mr. Ballard. Like Mother says, we won't stand in your way. After all, you're both adults. But, Mr. Ballard—"

"He has a first name, Dad. It's David."

"Yes. David. Mother and I would appreciate it if you would wait a few months. At least let a full year pass from Michelle's engagement to Scott."

David's facial muscles twitched. "A year?" As comprehension set in, he lost his composure completely. "A year, you say?"

"The year will be up in May," Dad said evenly. "That's just six months, Mr.—uh, David. If my daughter's worth waiting for . . ."

David slipped his arm around me as he assured my father, "Yes, Mr. Merrill, she's definitely worth waiting for, sir."

CHAPTER THREE

That evening David and I had dinner at the Cafe Gazelle, a charming little Italian bistro on Second Street, pleasant and unpretentious, with succulent *Bocconcini Marsala.*

Neither of us had much to say. We both felt subdued after our earlier conversation with my dad. I knew David didn't like the idea of someone else setting the guidelines for our relationship. He was his own man; it hadn't been easy for him to accept my father's stipulation on our marriage.

I was disappointed too. Devastated, in fact. For two weeks I had worried about whether David had marriage in mind. Now that we both knew it was what we wanted, waiting six months seemed anticlimactic, if not downright impossible.

"Your folks' reaction to my proposal really has you depressed," said David, reaching across the table for my hand.

"It's not just my folks."

"There's nothing that says we can't get engaged,"

he said seriously. "I want to give you a ring, Michelle."

"Oh, David, this isn't what you had in mind."

"I admit it won't be easy putting our relationship on hold for six months, but we'll manage. I'm not going to pressure you, Michelle, if that's what concerns you."

"No, David. If I seem preoccupied, it's because of other things. . . ."

"Other things? Problems?"

I looked away. I didn't want to tell him about my nightmares, but I had to share some of the dread I'd been feeling. "It—It's Morro Bay," I said haltingly. "The cocaine syndicate. I keep reliving the terror of it all. They almost killed us, David. Doesn't it still bother you?"

"Yes, I suppose it does." His lips tightened. The scar that traced his jawline pulsated slightly. "But I try not to dwell on it, Michelle. I spent enough years living with the horror of Vietnam."

I gazed down at my sauteed filet mignon and sweet peppers. Even now I could remember David's anguished words as he told me how his friend, Rob Thornton, had died in Vietnam: *I killed him as surely as if I'd aimed my revolver point-blank and fired.*

Searching David's eyes, I asked, "You don't still feel guilty, do you?"

"No, Michelle. You helped me work through my guilt in Morro Bay. But the events of the day Rob died—our Phantom crashing, the Vietnamese boy coming out of the jungle clutching a grenade, my hesitation to shoot him, then the thundering explosion . . ."

"You don't have to talk about it now, David."

"It's odd, Michelle. Even after all these years, I still

see it so clearly, bigger than life...the plane a ball of fire, the flames leapfrogging, Rob...Rob gone..."

"Please, David, don't do this to yourself. It wasn't your fault."

His expression softened. "I know, Michelle. But the memories of it are branded in my mind, as much a part of me as this scar on my chin."

"Rob is still very much in Eva's thoughts too," I noted.

"I know he is." David drummed his fingertips on the checkered oilcloth. "How can we forget, Michelle? People are talking about Vietnam again... finally. Ironically, the country's most unpopular war is no longer *verboten*."

"You're right," I acknowledged. "With all the movies and TV specials and newspaper headlines about Vietnam, I suppose it is difficult to put the past behind you."

"Don't get me wrong," said David. "I'm glad people are finally willing to talk about it. Vietnam Vets have waited much too long for a little recognition and consideration. But all the attention can't help but dredge up a lot of painful memories for us."

I nodded. There didn't seem to be much else to say. We finished our dinner with a minimum of small talk, then David drove me home to my tiny Costa Mesa apartment.

As he walked me to the door, he cautioned, "I don't like this neighborhood, Michelle. It's not safe for a woman living alone."

"I chose it for its price, David, not its exclusive location."

We went inside and David glanced around. "You mentioned there have been some robberies and break-ins in the area—"

"Yes, some," I admitted reluctantly. "But I'm more bothered by my neighbors' rowdy parties in the wee hours of the morning."

"Then, by all means, you should move."

"Where else could I get a furnished fourplex on a secretary's salary?"

David drew me into his arms. "You're not hitting the boss for a raise now, are you?"

"And if I were?"

"You just might get it," he said, kissing my hair and eyes.

I pulled back slightly. "Maybe I should get a roommate."

He kissed the nape of my neck. "You'll have one in six months."

"I mean now."

"I'd love to," he murmured, "but your folks would never go for it."

"I don't mean you, David. Maybe one of the girls from work." Lightly I added, "I hear Mitzi Piltz is looking for a roommate."

David chuckled bemusedly. "Yes, she's made that fact obvious to me on a number of occasions."

"Are you suggesting I should be jealous?"

"Not in a million years." David crushed me against him and silenced my question with his lips. I felt myself melting in his embrace.

"I can't hold you close enough," he murmured. Then, with a sigh, he released me. "If I don't leave now, I might not go at all," he said huskily.

"I—I feel the same way. One of us had better be strong."

He turned to the door. "This waiting is for the birds. I'd like to whisk you away to Vegas tonight."

"Is this the practical, conservative David Ballard speaking?" I teased.

He kissed my nose lightly and stepped out onto the porch. "Now you know why I kept my distance those two weeks after Morro Bay."

"What do you mean?"

"I mean, I had to keep a clear head while I prayed about God's will for us." He winked slyly. "I didn't want to be unduly influenced by the—what shall we say?—explosive passions you've stirred in me."

"Why, Mr. Ballard, you flatter me beyond words," I quipped in my breathy Scarlett O'Hara voice.

We both laughed, breaking the tension of the moment. "See you at the office, darling," he murmured softly.

"Love you," I whispered as I reluctantly shut the door between us.

After David left, I leaned against the door and listened to his Mercedes pulling away. My apartment rang with a wrenching emptiness. Already I missed him and yearned for his touch. It didn't feel right that he was going, leaving me behind. I felt lonely, incomplete. Nervously I turned out the living room lights and peeked through the venetian blinds. The neighborhood was surprisingly quiet tonight, the tree-lined street immersed in a shadowy darkness. I checked the lock again, then took the few steps to my tiny bathroom, showered quickly and dressed for bed.

As I slipped between the covers, I realized how exhausted I was—emotionally and physically. I tried to concentrate on sleep, but I was too tired to relax. A tree limb rustled slightly, scratching my window pane with an irritating rhythm. I wasn't one to count sheep, so I mentally traced David's features instead, but even thoughts of him didn't quell my anxieties.

I tried to pray, but even as the words formed they were snatched away by vivid images—a menacing figure from the cocaine syndicate pursuing me . . . Eva's son Rob Thornton consumed in flames beside his Phantom jet . . . David running wildly through the Vietnamese jungle, his jaw gaping open, bleeding profusely . . . .

At last I drifted into an uneasy sleep. My dreams came in bizarre fragments. David and I were crash-landing his Bonanza again, but now it was Vietnam and the plane erupted in flames. David kept shouting Rob's name. "Get Rob!" he told me. "Get Rob!" But I couldn't find him. Then Eva was there, weeping for her son, lamenting, "No one told him about God. No one told him!"

I reached out to both David and Eva, but they couldn't see me. Suddenly they were gone, and I was running alone through the jungle, breathless, pursued again by the cocaine syndicate. As I reached a clearing, I spotted the ocean. Suddenly, once again, I was a captive on the syndicate's fishing vessel. David was there. He embraced me. Then viciously my captors tore me from his arms and cast me overboard into the chilling waters of the Pacific. I sank into murky blackness as foaming waves surged over me. Then, incredibly, the waves became a swirling snowstorm of cocaine covering me like a shroud.

I awoke, damp with perspiration, and reached for the telephone. Trembling, I dialed David. He answered on the second ring. "David? It's Michelle."

"What's wrong?" He sounded groggy.

"I'm sorry to wake you, but you said I could call..."

"Another nightmare?"

"Yes. It was terrible, everything I've ever dreaded in one fell swoop—Morro Bay, Vietnam—"

"I'll be right over."

"David, no, it's too far. I can't ask you to—"

"I don't mind, Michelle. The freeways are clear at three a.m. I'll make good time."

"No, David, don't come."

"Why not?"

"I—I won't want you to go home again."

There was a pause. "You're right," he admitted. "I won't want to leave either."

"So it's more prudent for you to stay away in the first place," I mumbled, fighting my disappointment.

"Prudent," he reflected, "but surely no fun."

"I'll be all right now that I've talked to you, David. Go back to sleep, okay?"

"If you're sure. But I'm talking to Eva in the morning. It's time you had a roommate."

David was true to his word. When I arrived at work just before eight a.m., Eva was already emerging from David's office, her usual bright and buoyant self. "David and I had a long conversation, Michelle," she confided, "and now you and I need to talk."

"If it's about the nightmares—"

"It's about you moving in with me. It's David's idea, but the moment he suggested it, I knew it was the thing to do. So if you don't mind rooming with an old fogy like me..."

"Oh, Eva, I couldn't possibly impose on you like that!"

"Impose, nothing! You'd be doing me a favor. I just rattle around in that roomy condominium by myself. I'd love some company, and I can't think of anyone better than you."

I hesitated. "I'm not sure I could afford living in Irvine—"

"Oh, Michelle, don't worry. I already own the place. We'll just have monthly upkeep, utilities, and the homeowners association dues. In fact, you'll be able to save money for your wedding."

"Well, it would only be for six months," I reasoned, warming to the idea.

"You'll love it there at Windsong Cove, Michelle. My condo has a pool, spa, clubhouse, and tennis courts, not to mention jogging trails and a gated entrance that's locked at night. I feel completely safe there."

The gate cinched it for me. "Let's both think it over for a few days," I said, but I already knew my answer would be yes.

That weekend David helped me move my meager belongings—clothes, books, and knickknacks—into Eva's luxury Mediterranean-style condominium with its Spanish lace stucco and quaint red tile rooftops. The sprawling complex sat on a secluded hillside among several towering evergreens.

If I thought the landscaping was impressive, Eva's spacious, three-bedroom condo was even more elegant inside, with its cathedral ceiling, huge gourmet kitchen, and large, sun-filled rooms. The living room was tastefully furnished with a dark, Spanish decor and a gleaming baby grand piano.

Eva led me to my room at the end of the hall—a delightfully feminine alcove with lace and frills, a canopy bed and a delicate writing desk. On the east wall were built-in bookshelves and a pastel Degas print titled, *Dancer on Stage*. Looking around my lovely new surroundings, I felt as light and rhapsodic as the dancing ballerina in the painting.

Once Eva opened her door to welcome me, I was no longer just a guest. Her home was mine to share and enjoy. In some ways she was still the busy, efficient Eva Thornton I knew from the office. But in spite of our age difference, I soon discovered her to be an easy, fun-loving roommate. We jogged together each evening and took turns cooking the meals. I was eager to learn new recipes and special dishes for David, and Eva was glad to share her expertise in the kitchen.

Eva loved music, hummed a lot around the house, and played her piano for hours at a time. During our first few days together, we talked endlessly about good books and classical music and faraway places. I shared my dream of becoming a professional writer. We both planned to travel. Someday. We wondered when.

There was only one thing that puzzled me—Eva's strange obsession with the middle bedroom—the mysterious room she referred to as Rob's. She usually kept the door closed and insisted that nothing be disturbed. She explained cryptically, "Years ago when I came to California, I brought Rob's things with me. I wanted to keep his room exactly the way he had known it."

One Saturday while Eva was out with friends, I entered the room and gazed around curiously. The masculine furnishings were accented by collegiate trophies on the dresser, faded pennants lining the walls, and model airplanes suspended from the ceiling.

I shook my head in amazement. It seemed so unlike Eva to cling to the past. Once in a while she had mentioned her husband—fond little memories and anecdotes—but other than a large photo of him on her bedside table, there were no reminders of the elder Robert Thornton. She had buried him long ago.

But her son—that was different. The haunting, elusive aura of his room gave me the feeling that any day he'd be back to take possession. It gave me a weird sensation, standing there among his things. I wondered why Eva was trying to keep Rob alive when he had been gone so long.

I was so deep in contemplation that I didn't hear Eva come in. She slipped up behind me and asked quietly, "What are you doing in here, Michelle?"

"Oh, Eva—" I was embarrassed to be caught prying in Rob's room. "I'm sorry, I was just wondering why your son's room is . . ."

"Just like he left it?"

"I guess that's it." I was blundering through now. "Some people pack things away . . . try to forget, while you—"

"Surround myself with memories?" She walked over to his dresser and picked up a trophy. "Rob won this in college on the swim team." Her sigh filled the entire room. "He was so athletic, Michelle. So alive. So full of promise. I wish you could have known him."

I gazed up at Rob's snapshots tucked in the bureau mirror—a boyish, grinning youngster in a Cub Scout uniform, a lean muscular youth on the softball team, and a carefree college man in a letterman's jacket, surrounded by classmates and girlfriends.

"Rob looked so handsome in his tuxedo," said Eva,

pointing to another photo of a smiling, crinkly-eyed young man. "It was his first prom. He went with the same girl for two years. I still hear from her at Christmastime," Eva added with quiet pride.

Then, as she clasped a framed picture of Rob in his Navy uniform, she said, "This is the way Rob looked the last time I saw him—vibrant, brave, fearless. He told me not to worry." There was a tremor in her voice. "He even promised me he'd come home someday. And the whole time I kept thinking, 'Oh God, what if he doesn't?' "

I put a tentative, comforting hand on Eva's shoulder. There was nothing I could say or do, except to silently share her grief. I could see the tears glistening in Eva's eyes, but she held them back as she murmured, "Rob's father would have been so proud of him."

Curiosity gnawed at me, so I spoke, perhaps out of turn. "I can't help but notice, Eva. You have so little around that speaks of Rob's father."

Eva shook her head slowly. "Dear Robert," she sighed. "He died when Rob was a child. A sudden heart attack right in my arms and he was gone. I thought I'd never get over it, but for Rob's sake I picked up the pieces and went on." She shuddered involuntarily. "But when Rod died, there were no pieces to pick up."

That was it, I realized sadly. Eva had buried her husband. He had died in her arms, and she knew he was gone. But with Rob there was no body, no burial, no rituals of healing. As Eva had so aptly put it, with Rob's death there were no pieces to pick up.

CHAPTER
FOUR

On the first Saturday in December, Eva and I were in the kitchen baking for the Christmas holidays when the doorbell rang. "Can you catch that for me, Michelle?" she asked as she wiped her floury hands on her apron. "David hates burned cookies."

"No problem." I snatched up a warm sugar cookie and hurried to answer the persistent ringing.

I opened the door to a tall, dark, square-jawed stranger in a tan raincoat. He immediately tipped his visor cap to me, a cap that almost hid his shrewd, wide-spread hazel eyes. "Mrs. Thornton?" he asked pleasantly with a cunning half-smile.

"No, I'm Michelle."

"Well, good morning, Michelle. How are you?" As he removed his cap a gust of wind caught his unruly brown hair. He made a quick attempt to smooth it down.

Deep inside, I felt warning signs go up. *A salesman!* "I don't want to buy a thing," I said at once.

"I'm not selling anything," he answered cockily.

"I have good news for you and Mrs. Thornton."

"We get our news from the TV," I told him.

"It's not always *good* news on TV."

I was intrigued now but still prepared to slam the door for safety's sake, if need be.

"Now if you and your mother will just give me a minute of your time—"

"She's not my mother. We're friends. Roommates."

"Perhaps I should introduce myself..." He whipped out a magazine from his coat pocket and pointed his forefinger at a lead article: "Tracking American Servicemen: A Humanitarian Issue," by Lance Edwards.

"I gather you're Lance Edwards."

"The same. Go ahead. Read the article."

Another warning signal went up. I didn't care for this man's reckless indifference or his haughty manner. "I don't like reading on the porch any better than I like salesmen."

"I promise you, I'm not a salesman. I'm a freelance reporter."

"Not interested," I answered flatly, although my writer's curiosity was piqued.

"If you're not interested, how can I do an article on the Thornton family?"

"What makes you think they have a story?" I asked, playing along.

"I just returned from Thailand, following up a news lead—I helped unearth a little nugget that came over the wires of the Associated Press..."

"The wrong nugget," I suggested.

He scowled. "I assure you I'm really very thorough. I've traveled to Southeast Asia a number of times. I've been hitting the MIA issue for several years and figured I could get an interview with Mrs. Thornton—you know, from the family angle. I don't mind admitting I thrive on controversial subjects."

"You're really crazy, Mr. Edwards. Really."

"I still have good news for you," he said brashly.

I couldn't resist. "Go on."

"Surely you saw the news flash on TV this morning."

"I haven't been listening to the TV. We're baking cookies."

He sniffed deeply. "I know."

I started to shut the door.

"Wait," he urged. "It's quite possible the news affects you."

My throat constricted. *Not David!* "What are you talking about?" I asked anxiously.

"The MIA report."

I frowned. "I don't know anyone missing in action."

"Then call it POW. It's about Lt. Rob Thornton."

I froze. "That's cruel."

"I thought you'd be glad to hear—"

"Rob Thornton is dead," I whispered, hoping that Eva wouldn't overhear me. "My fiance saw him die. Rob Thornton has been dead for years."

Lance Edwards looked momentarily uncertain. He took out a notepad and scrutinized it, then said with a shrug, "My apologies. Perhaps I have the wrong address."

I walked slowly back to the kitchen, grateful that Eva had been too busy to answer the door. She didn't need to be involved in a vicious hoax or hear a misinformed reporter spreading false rumors.

"Well," said Eva, "what was that all about?"

"I guess I really didn't find out."

"What was he selling? Magazines?"

"I never gave him time to tell me."

Eva pulled on her oven mitt. "Well, you got rid of him. Now I know who to send to the door the next time a salesman calls."

I picked up a cookie and nibbled it uneasily.

Eva slid another baking sheet into the oven. "I'm sunk if David doesn't like my cookies any better than that," she teased.

"Oh, he'll love them," I said, brightening. "Just wait'll he tastes them after dinner tonight."

"Speaking of dinner, you'd better get the steaks out of the freezer, Michelle."

The idea of preparing dinner for David lifted my spirits and took my mind off the rude, ingratiating reporter. I was determined to make this one of the best meals David had ever eaten. I wanted him to be assured that his future wife was also an excellent cook. Not that I was all that confident in the kitchen, but Eva was doing her best to teach me, and I was an eager learner.

That evening everything was perfect when David arrived. We sat down to a scruptious dinner at a candlelit table decorated with Eva's best china and silver. David was obviously impressed. "Who do I thank for this extraordinary dinner?" he asked as he held out his plate for a second helping.

"Michelle, of course," said Eva quickly.

"And Eva," I added. "I couldn't have done it without her help."

"You two make quite a team," noted David. "And if I keep eating like this, I'll have to jog an extra couple of miles every morning."

"And you haven't even seen the dessert yet," I said, pushing back my chair. I went to the kitchen and returned with a silver platter of Eva's fancily decorated Christmas cookies and frosty goblets of raspberry sherbet.

David and Eva were reminiscing about their early days together. "Even when it looked like we'd lose everything, we settled for peanut butter sandwiches to keep the business going," chuckled David.

Eva looked up at me as I set the tray on the table. "You know, Michelle, between David's savvy and my stubbornness, we made the company go. Did you know we started it all in a one-room office not much bigger than this room?"

"No, I didn't."

David smiled. "I couldn't have asked for a better business partner than Eva."

"Well, I got a son out of the deal!" chimed Eva. Then she gazed fondly at me. "And soon I'll have a dear daughter-in-law. It's almost as if my son Rob had lived to bring home a fiancee." She blinked back sudden tears and sighed, "Life is good."

"If only we didn't have to wait another five months for our wedding," mused David, taking my hand.

Eva put her hand over both of ours. "You two remember this. In years to come you'll be happy you waited for her parents' blessing." Eva's eyes moistened again as she assured us, "You already have mine."

"You know, the three of us make quite a family," I said softly. "You both make me feel as if I really belong."

"You do," agreed David. "And soon we'll belong to each other. Which reminds me. There's something else we need to talk about."

"Perhaps you should tell me over dessert," I

suggested. "Your sherbet's melting."

"All right," said David cagily, taking one of the icy goblets. "Maybe you're not interested in talking about a ring."

"A ring?" I blurted. "Why didn't you say so?"

"I'm trying to," he laughed. "I was just wondering, do you want to go shopping with me? Or would you like to be surprised?"

"Oh, David, I—"

Before I could finish my reply, the telephone rang.

"Now who could that be?" said Eva, not moving. "I'm not expecting any calls."

"We're all here," I quipped.

"Shall I get it, Eva?" David offered.

"No. Finish your sherbet. And your conversation."

Eva went to the buffet, picked up the receiver and emitted a formal hello. "Yes, this is Eva Thornton. . . ."

"So what do you think?" David asked me quietly. "Are you going with me to buy the ring?"

"Oh, you've caught me so off guard, I—"

"Who are you?" said Eva sharply. I saw her grasp the edge of the buffet. "What kind of joke is this?" she cried.

David looked up quizzically. "Who is it, Eva?"

She covered the mouthpiece. Her voice wavered. "They say it's Washington—the Pentagon."

"The Pentagon?"

"What?" Eva said into the receiver. "Yes, I had a son, but he died years ago in Vietnam, at the close of the war. Pardon? You say Robert A. Thornton, Jr.? Yes, that was his name."

I tensed with alarm. "David, it must be that reporter who came today—"

"Reporter? What are you talking about?"

"Oh, the man was absolutely batty—and fishing for a story. I thought I got rid of him—"

Eva sank down into the nearest chair. Her hand holding the receiver shook violently. She gazed up starkly at David, all color drained from her face. "He says—he told me Rob is alive—"

David pushed back his chair, strode over and snatched the phone from Eva. "Who is this?" he demanded. He was silent for a minute, but the muscles in his face grew taut and his mouth twitched involuntarily. "There must be some mistake," he said in a low, precise voice. "I was with him when he died. I saw it. Our F-4 Phantom was blown to bits. There was no way he could have survived."

I went over and slipped my arm around David, giving him my silent support. He was trembling. "You say he was blown away from the wreckage... wounded...captured?"

Eva was weeping now. I handed her David's handkerchief.

"Where has he been all these years?" David was saying, still sounding unconvinced. "A prisoner of war? Why in blazes wasn't he found until now? All right, you can fill us in on the details later. Just tell us what to do."

Eva clutched David's hand. "Is it true? Is my son really alive?"

"It looks quite possible," David uttered, barely controlling his own mounting emotions. He spoke in low, sober tones a few more minutes, then hung up the phone and turned to Eva. Dropping on one knee, he took both her hands in his. "They say there's no mistake. It's Rob. He's coming home."

The two of them embraced and wept. Then,

through her tears, Eva bombarded David with questions. "Is my son all right? When will he be home? Where did they find him?"

"The information is sketchy right now, Eva. Rob was found at a refugee camp in Thailand. He had apparently been living in a Laotian village for several years. Before that he was a prisoner of war. Somehow he escaped. He's going to need hospital care, but they seem to think he'll be all right."

"Oh, thank God!" she breathed. "When can I see him?"

"He'll be spending a few days at Clark Air Force Base in the Philippines for medical treatment and debriefing. Then the Navy will fly him to the Naval Hospital in San Diego."

"Then he must be hurt—"

"He'll need care, Eva, but they assured me it's nothing life-threatening. We'll drive to San Diego to meet him."

Eva covered her mouth with her hands. Tears streamed down her cheeks. "Oh, David, is it really possible? After all these years? Rob coming home? My baby coming home?"

"I can't believe it myself," said David.

I hugged Eva. "He'll be here in time for Christmas!"

Eva's expression grew vibrant, alive. "Rob—home for the holidays. Oh, Michelle, dear, there's so much to do!"

"Yes, but I'll help you, and oh, it'll be such fun—!"

I looked around and realized that David had left the room. I heard him in the bathroom, coughing. Eva and I exchanged wordless glances. Then we heard the terrible sound of great, racking sobs. Neither of us spoke or moved. We both sensed that this was something David had to work through alone.

Eva and I went to the living room. She picked up Rob's portrait from the piano and cradled it against her breast. We sat down on the sofa and waited, talking in hushed tones like two people caught in a dream, suspended between fantasy and reality. A stranger on the phone had said Rob was alive. But it would take time for a handful of words to cancel out a dozen years of grief.

Over an hour later David returned to us. For an instant I didn't recognize him. There were so many new emotions in his face I'd never seen before. But I could tell by his expression that he had fought a different kind of war in his soul and had come through intact. He was ready now to lend Eva the support she needed.

The three of us talked until midnight, marveling, making plans, and praising God for this most unexpected of miracles. David left reluctantly, as if parting might somehow break the spell and negate the incredible news about Rob.

Neither Eva nor I slept that night except in fitful snatches. We were up and down, passing in the hallway, sitting in the darkened kitchen sipping cups of hot tea. Early the next morning I awoke to the sounds of muffled voices outside and car doors slamming shut. I pulled on my blue velour robe and hurried to the living room. Eva stood by the bay window, already dressed in slacks and a long-sleeved silk blouse. "Come here, Michelle," she said softly. "We're not the only ones rejoicing over Rob."

I went over and gave her a quick hug. Her eyelids were swollen, but there was a beautiful light in her eyes. She nodded toward the front yard.

I peeked through the sheer curtains. The Channel 4 Mobile Unit was there. Several reporters milled around on the lawn, waiting, their portable video cameras poised on their shoulders.

Then I spotted the exasperating reporter from yesterday—Lance somebody—standing off to one side of the crowd, wearing the same tan, all-weather coat, his visor cap pushed back jauntily on his head.

"Rejoicing?" I echoed skeptically. "They look more like vultures ready to seize their prey."

Eva smiled wanly. "We'll give them the benefit of the doubt, Michelle. I've called David. He'll know how to handle the crowds and the reporters. I'd only cry."

"They should leave you alone at a time like this," I said indignantly.

"No, Michelle. Rob's coming home from Vietnam after all these years is news. We have to share it. And," she added meaningfully, "we have to face the fact that our lives are never going to be the same."

"I suppose you're right, Eva." I gazed back out the window, wondering uneasily in just what earth-shaking ways Rob's return would change all of our lives.

CHAPTER
FIVE

Ten days later, a brisk December wind whipped against us as we stood in the open field at Miramar Naval Air Station waiting for Rob's C-9 *Nightingale* to arrive. It was dusk, with a pastel wash of pinks and blues brushing the horizon. I pressed close to David, tightening my clasp on his arm, savoring the warmth of his nubby overcoat.

Eva stood a few feet away, small and fragile beside the tall, barrel-chested Commander in his dress blues. A thick-jowled man with an aquiline nose and a compelling smile, Commander Thomas spoke in no-nonsense tones. "I assure you, Mrs. Thornton, your son's plane will be on time. They left Travis Air Force Base forty minutes ago."

"Are you sure he's all right?" Eva fretted.

"We've been in touch with the Med-evac team ever since they left Clark Air Force Base in the Philippines," replied the officer. "They say Lt. Thornton is resting comfortably."

The worry lines in Eva's face deepened. "I

49

watched the plane take off on the TV newscast yesterday, but when they carried my son on board on a stretcher, they didn't show a closeup of his face. I can't help wondering if something's wrong—"

"He's in good hands, Mrs. Thornton." The Commander spoke over the roar of Navy jets landing and taking off on the airstrip nearby.

"But it's been such a long trip, with layovers in Guam and Hawaii," said Eva. "Rob must be exhausted by now."

The Commander's expression remained stolid. "The layovers are necessary, ma'am, for refueling and picking up other military patients."

"But they tell me my son has cerebral malaria. Is it safe for him to travel such a long distance?"

"The doctors wouldn't have released Lt. Thornton from Clark if he hadn't been stabilized. Besides, the *Nightingale*, as well as the C-141 that carried him from the Philippines to Travis, is well equipped for medical emergencies."

"Rob has his own physician and a complete nursing staff traveling with him, Eva," interjected David. "He'll be on top of the world with all that attention."

"That's my boy," smiled Eva faintly. "He always loved being the life of the party."

"Well, now he has the love and attention of the entire country," I reminded her.

"That's certainly true," the Commander agreed. "I've given the order to keep the reporters and TV crews at bay until you've had a chance to greet your son. But it's like keeping back a hungry pack of wolves."

"And I know the leader of the pack," I told David confidentially. "That Lance Edwards has been at the house every day. He's bound and determined to do a cover story on Rob."

"Isn't he the fellow who got wind of the news before Eva did?"

"Right. He was in Thailand when Rob was found. I have a feeling he'd sell his own mother's soul to get this story."

Commander Thomas stepped over beside David and said, "As soon as the three of you have had a few minutes to greet Lt. Thornton, our Med-evac bus will transport him directly to the Naval Hospital. We'll follow in my vehicle."

"Then you plan to bypass the media?"

He nodded. "The Public Affairs Office will handle all publicity. For now it's essential to restrict news coverage until Lt. Thornton undergoes further debriefing at the hospital."

"But my son's already been questioned in the Philippines."

"It's routine, Mrs. Thornton. In your son's case, it's possible he may know of other MIA's . . ."

"Commander Thomas is right, Eva. There may be more men out there just like Rob," David explained. "If there's the slightest chance that others are alive, the State Department needs to know."

"It's all still so incredible," murmured Eva. "I feel as if I'll wake up at any moment and realize it's all a dream—"

David reached over and embraced her. "It's the same for me, Eva," he replied, his voice tender with emotion.

Eva removed a handkerchief from her purse and dabbed her eyes. "I feel so nervous, David. I wasn't even this tense and anxious the day Rob was born." She looked imploringly from David to me. "Do you think he'll remember me? Will he still be my Rob?"

I hugged her impulsively, my arms circling David as well. "Oh, Eva, of course he'll remember you!"

"But they mentioned symptoms of amnesia . . . mental confusion. They said I should be *prepared*. But I don't know what that means."

I didn't have the answer any more than Eva did, but I felt an overwhelming need to reassure her. I wanted this to be the happiest day of her life. "The relationship between a mother and son—that's something special," I said persuasively. "I'm sure Rob has kept you first in his heart all these years."

Eva looked to David for confirmation. "Will he be the same, David? The worst thing I can imagine is that after all these years he'll be a stranger to us. I couldn't bear that."

David gently pressed Eva's head against his chest. "Rob has been through a lot," he said. "We'll have to help him find his way back. We've got to be strong for him."

Eva smiled through her tears. "I still picture a sturdy, bright-eyed boy of twenty. That's how he's looked to me all these years."

Eva's words were swallowed by a high, shrill noise overhead.

"Here she comes," announced the Commander.

We gazed in awed silence as the sleek, white C-9 *Nightingale* burst through the darkness like a huge phantom ship. The plane swooped from the sky with an eagle's grace, then touched down with a jarring, grating noise as her wheels spun searingly against concrete. I spotted the bright Red Cross insignia emblazoned on her tail as the aircraft rolled to a smooth stop hardly a hundred feet from us.

"They'll bring your son off first," Commander Thomas told us.

After several minutes, the aircraft's massive side doors opened wide and a long ramp unraveled before us. Several military personnel emerged, followed by two nurses. Eva stood between David and me, spellbound, gripping our arms with a fierceness that almost made me flinch. I had a feeling that if we let her go, she would collapse.

Finally we spotted the wheelchair. A corpsman pushed it carefully down the ramp. I wished I could take out my writer's notebook and capture the moment in words: *A frail windlestraw of a man sat in the chair shrouded in shadows.*

The blue haze of the airport lights cut across Rob's features. It was glimpse enough to prompt a sob low in Eva's throat. She broke away from us and ran. Suddenly we were all running. Everything was happening at once. Eva pushed past the medical attendants and fell upon the form in the chair, embracing him, weeping, running her hands over his bearded face as if sight alone were not enough to make him real to her.

For a moment my heart lurched in alarm. The man made no attempt to return Eva's embrace. He sat slumped and forlorn, his arms listless and unmoving. *Respond!* I wanted to shout. *She's waited twelve years for you!*

Slowly the man looked up. The harsh airport lights profiled his gaunt features, his hollow, deepset eyes. Even though I had warned myself not to expect the smiling, rosy-cheeked boy from Eva's old photographs, I felt a wave of shock wash over me. For an instant I thought of wrenching pictures I'd seen of concentration camp victims from World War II. *We're in for a long, hard journey*, I reflected, and immediately felt guilty for my selfish reaction.

Eva was murmuring over and over, "Rob, my son, my precious boy! It's Mother!"

After a moment Rob's eyes fixed on her with a smoldering intensity. I heard him utter, half in question, "Mother?" Then his hands unfolded mechanically as he reached out to touch her.

"Darling, you're home. Almost home."

David bent over Rob too, extending an awkward hand, gripping the bony fingers. "Buddy," he managed. The sound he made was more like a sob.

Rob gazed up quizzically and opened his mouth as if to speak.

"Rob, it's me—David—your old Navy buddy." David's face contorted with an anguish I'd never seen before. "David Ballard, remember? Last time I saw you was when our Phantom crashed in Nam."

Bewilderment flickered in Rob's eyes.

"I thought you were dead, man." David fought for control. "I thought the grenade got you. But, thank God, you were thrown clear."

Rob struggled for words. "Sometimes I feel the explosion in my head—a terrible brightness, blinding, splitting my skull—"

"You're right, Rob. The plane—everything—was in flames."

"I can't remember the plane—"

"Later, man," said David kindly. "It's over now. We'll talk about it later." He turned and drew me over beside him. "I want you to meet my fiancee, Michelle Merrill."

Rob stared up at me with intense, probing eyes. He had a fragile face with chiseled features, high cheekbones, a curly beard and light mustache. A shock of wavy brown hair cascaded over his forehead.

I took his hand in mine. "Hello, Rob."

"Liana?" For a moment his fingers wrapped around mine, tenderly, desperately. "You came back, Liana," he said again with a strange yearning.

"No. I'm *Michelle*, Rob."

His hand slipped away, falling limply into his lap. I felt an inexplicable disappointment, as if somehow I had failed this brooding, inscrutable stranger.

Commander Thomas stepped forward and said, "Lt. Thornton, we'll have to board you on the Med-evac bus for the hospital."

"Who's Thornton?" Rob echoed with a hint of puzzlement. "The name's Cory Rugby, sir."

"Lieutenant, your family will meet you at the hospital." The Commander nodded hastily to the corpsman nearby.

"Cory Rugby?" I questioned under my breath. I looked at Eva, but she was watching the corpsman swing Rob's wheelchair around and push it swiftly to the bus. We waited in silence until the vehicle was out of sight.

Eva was shivering now. The Commander put a steadying hand on her elbow. "Is something wrong, Mrs. Thornton?"

"Wrong?" She squeezed out the words through taut lips. "You already know, don't you, Commander? My son doesn't even know me."

Without reply the Commander guided her toward his car. David and I followed.

I was overwhelmed, my emotions heightened to the point of exhaustion. I couldn't understand what was happening. Who was Cory Rugby? And why would Rob make such a claim?

As David climbed into the back seat beside me, I glanced at his face. His jaw was clenched, his eyes oddly troubled. I knew he had been deeply touched by Rob's gaunt body and haunted expression, but this was something else, an elusive pain etched in David's countenance. Wordlessly I clasped his hand. He turned his gaze to the window, shutting me out.

"It'll be all right," I whispered.

All he could do was nod.

CHAPTER
SIX

Leaving the Miramar Naval Air Station, Commander Thomas headed his vehicle south on Highway 163 at a leisurely pace toward the hospital. Finally breaking our numb silence, he said, "Lt. Thornton should be settled comfortably in his room by the time we get there."

"No red tape?" David asked.

"As little as possible. They'll be taking him right to his room."

Eva spoke up, her voice tremulous. "Commander, you warned us about Rob's amnesia. Why didn't you tell us he doesn't even know who he is?"

"Frankly, Mrs. Thornton, we had hoped his memory would return when he saw you."

David leaned forward. "Who's this Cory Rugby?"

"He's one of our MIA's—a captain in the Marine Corps."

"Why would Rob think he's this other man Rugby?" Eva persisted.

"Mrs. Thornton, the answer to that is locked deep

inside your son. Once we know, we may learn the whereabouts of Captain Rugby." There was a quiet sadness as he added, "Or we'll be able to close his file. The Rugbys have waited many years for information on their boy." In a lighter tone, he asked, "Tell me, Mrs. Thornton, how do you think your son looks?"

Eva shook her head. "Rob looks so tired, so thin, so—so old," she said softly. "I never would have recognized him."

"Who could with that curly beard of his?" returned David.

"The beard's not exactly regulation," remarked the Commander pleasantly. "But for now . . ."

"I rather like it myself," I offered.

"Oh, Michelle, Rob was such a strapping, clean-shaven boy, but now he looks so gaunt and haggard —like walking death—" Eva's words were lost in a gripping sob.

The Commander glanced over at her. "Do your crying now, Mrs. Thornton," he said kindly. "Save your smiles for the Lieutenant. He'll need all the strength you can give him."

"What are the plans, Commander?" questioned David. "When can we take Rob home?"

"He'll be undergoing extensive medical evaluations for the next few days."

"Then he won't be released tomorrow?" cried Eva.

"No, but we've set up a tentative family conference for tomorrow afternoon. Can you all be there?"

"A conference, sir?" echoed David. "What's that all about?"

The Commander swung his automobile onto Park Boulevard before answering. "We'll be briefing you on what little we know about your son's years in

Vietnam and his escape to Laos. We'll also discuss his rehabilitation program and how you can contribute to his readjustment to society."

"The best thing for Rob is being home for Christmas," exclaimed Eva. "It's his favorite time of year. He always loved decorating the tree and making little gifts for everyone. And, oh, he devoured Christmas cookies by the dozens." She sighed blissfully, remembering. "Oh, Commander Thomas, we simply must have my son home by Christmas!"

"We'll see what we can do about that, Mrs. Thornton."

"Speaking of Christmas," I chimed in, "look at the beautiful lights on those towers ahead."

"Miss Merrill, you're looking at the decorations on the twin towers of our Administration Building."

"You mean, this is the San Diego Naval Hospital? It's huge!" I gazed in fascination at the sprawling complex of Spanish-style buildings that crowned Balboa Park's Inspiration Point.

"Just wait'll we complete the new facility," said Commander Thomas. "We'll be the biggest, most modern military hospital in the world. In the meantime we may look a bit old-fashioned, but we've got full capability."

"Oh, I love it!" I told him buoyantly. "With all the little wrought iron balconies and quaint Hispanic bric-a-brac, you've captured a little piece of history."

"We *made* history," noted the Commander. "We began back in 1922 with bed space for fewer than 300 people. But during Christmas of 1944 our patient load reached a peak of 12,000."

"And all I care about," said Eva in a small, abashed voice, "is one lone patient."

"You'll be seeing him again in a few moments," Commander Thomas assured her.

We drove past a flower-studded chain-link fence, through the high iron gates, to a small guard house. The Commander returned a salute to the young sentry on duty, then drove up a slight incline toward the Administration Building. He parked in his private space across the street, then escorted us into the nondescript entryway to the main desk.

"If you'll excuse me, I'll check and see if they're ready for us," the Commander told Eva.

While we waited, we gazed absently at the detailed model of the new hospital—a charming array of miniature white structures. The Commander was back within moments. He led us out the back door, through a sprawling courtyard into the next building, then up an ancient, groaning elevator and across a narrow, enclosed catwalk to the main hospital.

"This is Building 26," he explained as we looked around at the drab, colorless lobby. "We call our hospital the 'Gray Ghost.' "

Silently I agreed with this somber appellation. The entire place possessed the muted, melancholy atmosphere of a museum piece. After a moment we took the elevator upstairs and followed Commander Thomas down a wide, utilitarian hallway toward an expansive ward at the end of the corridor.

"Is Rob in Open Bay?" asked David.

"No. He's getting the V.I.P. treatment—semi-private accommodations. Actually, he'll be the only patient occupying the room." He gestured toward an inauspicious cubicle just two doors short of the ward. "I'll leave the three of you alone with Lt. Thornton. When you're ready to go, a hospital corpsman will drive you to your motel."

We thanked the Commander, then, with an unexpected reticence, we entered Rob's room. I caught a glimpse of bland walls and an empty bed and table before my eyes settled on Rob in the bed by the window. He was dressed in hospital garb— light blue pajamas and a Navy pinstripe bathrobe. He lay propped up, his right leg elevated on pillows and his long, lean hands clasped in his lap.

His eyes were on us from the moment we stepped through the doorway—intense, poignant, icy blue- green. His lashes were thick and dark, giving his gaze a smoldering, veiled aura. His classic features were accentuated by his thinness—high, sculpted cheekbones, arched brows, a narrow, prominent nose, and finely carved lips.

I thought of all the photos of Rob I'd seen at Eva's home—Rob at his high school graduation, Rob at twenty on his college campus, Rob smiling proudly in his Navy uniform. Even a vivid writer's imagi- nation like mine found it difficult to subtract sixty pounds, add twelve years, and etch into his facial features the years of torment, torture, and loneli- ness from prison camps. What was once a hand- some, full, youthful face was now wasted and jaundiced. Rob was a hollow-cheeked, timeworn man in his early thirties. The boy in him was gone.

I watched Eva walk tentatively to Rob's bedside, bend over, and kiss his cheek. He reached out awkwardly, his fingers lingering on her face. "I don't remember you," he murmured, "but I wish I did. You look beautiful."

Eva struggled for control. "Oh, Rob, darling, you're a flatterer just like your dad."

Rob's brows raised quizzically. "Dad? Is he here?"

Eva looked stunned. She stared helplessly at David

and me. I shrugged. David nodded.

Eva sat down in the chair by Rob's bed and took his hand. "Don't you remember, honey? Daddy's been gone for a long time."

Rob's eyes clouded. "I can't remember him...."

"He died when you were just a little boy."

"He left us...when we needed him?" Rob's voice was vague, confused.

"Your dad didn't want to leave us—"

Rob's expression grew distant, impassive. Then, after a moment, his eyes brightened as they focused again on Eva. "You are so pretty. When they told me about you at Clark, I kept trying to picture you in my mind. But you look—you're different—better—so real—"

"Even with my wrinkles and grey-streaked hair?"

"It's shiny, nice, like Liana's—" A half smile crossed his face.

Eva stroked his hand soothingly, then stared with alarm at his fingertips. "You've been hurt, darling!"

He gazed at his rough, scarred fingers. "They said my hands were burned in the explosion—"

David stepped forward and gripped Rob's shoulder. "I wish to heaven I'd known you survived that exploding grenade," he said disconsolately.

"I didn't know about the grenade myself," replied Rob. His voice wandered. "But sometimes at night I catch glimpses of that miserable prison camp."

"It's all right, man," David said, his voice resonant with pain.

It was as though Rob never heard him. "They kept us in isolation," he mumbled to himself. "In cold, cramped cells or little thatched huts—dirty, stinking pigsties."

Eva began to weep. "My son, you've been through so much."

"Ma—Mom, I'm okay."

"But they told me you had cerebral malaria—"

"It's better. No more headaches—the chills are gone."

"But you look so—so—"

"I get confused, that's all. I forget. The doctor at Clark said it takes awhile—"

"We'll be here with you, son. You'll never be alone again."

He looked around the barren room. "I want to go home," he said softly. "I've dreamed of finding my real home for such a long time."

There was a mixture of anguish and joy in Eva's eyes. I wondered, Was Rob waiting for her to tell him she had dreamed of the same thing? Did he understand that she had believed him dead all these years?

Eva wept unashamedly now. "You will go home, my son. You'll be home for Christmas."

"Christmas?" he echoed. "Having a mother—that's Christmas for me." With exquisite tenderness he cupped her face in his bony hands and kissed her tears.

I looked away, feeling suddenly like a stranger invading the private sanctuary of their very souls. It was as if Eva and Rob were touched by the holy hush of angels hovering over them. For all of these years Eva had mourned the fact that her son had died without Christ, without redemption. Now it was as if he had stepped back from the brink of hell itself. Eva had the second chance she had always yearned for—a chance to tell her son of saving grace.

We spent a few more minutes with Rob. Then a

nurse slipped in with his medication and whispered confidentially, "Lt. Thornton has a long day tomorrow. He needs his rest."

"Nothing for Rugby?" Rob asked.

"Rugby—Thornton—whatever," she said, looking at his nameband. "The medicine's yours."

Rob shook his head as the nurse left the room. "She told me earlier I might as well get used to the name Rob Thornton." He raised one eyebrow at Eva. "Thornton, that's your name, right?"

"It's your name, too, Rob."

Reluctantly we said good night and assured Rob we would be back in the morning.

We returned to Building 26 early the next day. As we walked through the main lobby, I spotted Lance Edwards making his way toward us. "Trouble," I whispered to David. "Here comes that pushy news reporter again."

"I thought all publicity about Rob was being channeled through the PAO."

"The what?"

"The Public Affairs Office."

"Apparently everybody knows that except Lance Edwards," I quipped dryly.

David pushed the elevator button, but Edwards had already caught up with us. He feigned a polite bow to Eva. "Mrs. Thornton," he said, his voice dripping honey, "may I talk with you a minute?"

David answered for her. "Not now, sir. Later."

The elevator arrived. David guided Eva inside. I squeezed in behind them. Lance Edwards blocked the closing door with his shoulder. Tipping his hat to Eva, he persisted, "I believe I could be of help, Mrs. Thornton . . ."

"You can help by leaving us alone," David answered curtly.

Edwards gave David a coolly appraising glance. "It's a good thing I had a visit with the Lieutenant before you arrived. Tell me, how do you explain the fact that he claims to be Captain Cory Rugby?"

There was a smirk on his face as he stepped aside, allowing the elevator door to slam shut.

"Goodness, that's a persistent young man, David," Eva said quietly.

"We've been trying to cut Lance Edwards off for days now," I said. "But he's determined to write a story about Rob's homecoming."

"Well, we've certainly got a story to tell," she replied as we approached Rob's room. I noted that the night's rest had helped Eva. She was ready to tackle a new day, anything for her son.

But our time with Rob was all too brief and strangely unsatisfying—quick snatches of conversation among the endless tests and evaluations scheduled for him. Rob had just arrived back in his room for a late lunch when it was time for us to meet with Commander Thomas.

At two o'clock sharp we were seated in the Commander's office. Even though I wasn't actually "family," Eva had insisted I be there too. It felt good to be included. The Commander introduced us to two other officers—slim, sandy-haired Chaplain Crawford with a clipped Eastern accent, and the more serious, dark-eyed Captain Wickman, Chief of Medical Staff from Rob's floor.

Commander Thomas looked startlingly different without his familiar military headgear. He had a high forehead and thinning gray hair, giving him an exposed, vulnerable quality. I liked him better for it. After making introductions, he turned and addressed Eva in a careful, articulate voice. "While Lt. Thornton was at Clark, we received only sketchy bits of information, Mrs. Thornton. Even with what little we know, we still aren't at liberty to share everything." He smiled to reassure her. "Much will have to remain classified. Do you understand?"

"I think so," Eva answered. "Actually, I guess I don't really understand . . ."

He nodded. "Your son is the first POW to be released in a very long time. Do you realize what significance that has for our entire nation? If one man has survived this long, then there could be others. It's obvious that Lt. Thornton must have known Captain Rugby." The Commander cleared his throat and sat back in his chair. "We hope that as we treat your son's amnesia, he'll recall the whereabouts of Rubgy and perhaps other MIA's as well."

"Even if Rob supplies the information, would the Vietnamese government allow a search?" asked David.

"Periodically," Commander Thomas answered, "almost as a token courtesy, the Vietnamese government has returned the remains of some of our servicemen. And recently there have been some search teams permitted in Laos and Vietnam to scout the crash sites of our downed aircraft."

"I assume," said David, "you don't want to disturb the fragile balance in our diplomatic relations."

"Precisely," nodded the Commander.

"What can you tell us about Rob's captivity, sir?"

"Well, Mr. Ballard, from what we can piece together, after the shootdown of your Phantom jet, Lt. Thornton was taken captive by the North

Vietnamese. After the U.S. pulled out of Saigon in '75, he may have been interned with the thousands of South Vietnamese in what were euphemistically called 'reeducation camps.' We suspect that he made several escape attempts before finally succeeding. He made it into Laos, probably not knowing that that country, too, had fallen to the Communists. With his experience as a navigator, he may have tried to reach the Mekong River, hoping to cross into Thailand and freedom." The Commander was silent for a moment, choosing his words cautiously. "But the Mekong River was heavily patrolled by Communist Laotian soldiers, so there would have been little opportunity to escape."

"You mean, he was imprisoned again?" cried Eva.

"Our information is hazy, Mrs. Thornton. We believe he was with other Americans, perhaps MIA's." The Commander's brow furrowed. "We do know that he was befriended by the Hmong tribal people and lived among them for a number of years."

"The Hmong? Who are they?" I asked.

"A mountain people who migrated from China to Laos, Cambodia, and Vietnam centuries ago."

David rubbed his chin thoughtfully. "I'm surprised they were willing to risk hiding an American serviceman for so long."

"It's typical of them," replied the Commander. "In fact, during the Vietnam War the CIA recruited the Hmong to fight the North Vietnamese and the Pathet Lao Communists."

"They must be a very brave people," I remarked.

"Yes, and Lt. Thornton was evidently quite content to dwell among them," said Captain Wickman. "In fact, that may be the very reason he survived so long."

"What else do you know about these people?" asked Eva.

The Commander hesitated. "We do know there was a girl—a young woman from the Hmong village."

The Chaplain leaned forward. "She may have meant a great deal to the Lieutenant. We do know that he seemed deeply troubled when we asked about her."

The Commander continued. "The Lieutenant seems to think that she deserted him. Ran out when he needed her. Actually, she may have saved his life."

Eva twisted her handkerchief in her lap. "How?" she asked intently. "How did she save my son's life?"

The Commander glanced at Captain Wickman. He took the cue. "Cerebral malaria can be devastating, even fatal. Your son was undoubtedly wracked with high fever and delirium. This young woman apparently thought he would die untreated in her village unless she risked her life to save him. With the help of several villagers, she spirited Lt. Thornton across the patrolled Mekong River, safely out of Laos into a refugee camp in Thailand."

Commander Thomas added, "There are a number of refugee camps along the Thai border. They are filled with Cambodians, Vietnamese, and Laotians who have trekked through jungles and crossed mountains and rivers to freedom—always at great risk to their own lives. Once in the camp, Lt. Thornton, with his Caucasian features, was quickly suspected of being a missing American airman. When that fact became apparent, the political lines of communication blew wide open."

"That's right," interjected Captain Wickman.

"After about 72 hours of red tape, your son was flown to Clark Air Force Base."

"And the girl?" Eva asked, her voice barely audible.

"She stayed by Lt. Thornton's bedside at the refugee camp for several hours, but once she was assured they were doing all they could for him, she disappeared."

"Do you have any idea where she went?" I questioned, my mind whirling with the intrigue of it all.

"She could still be in the refugee camp, lost in the crowd," replied the Captain.

"Or she could be back across the Mekong River," the Commander suggested. "Back with her own people."

"Then I can never thank her," Eva said softly.

The Commander smiled at her. "You have a gentle spirit, Mrs. Thornton. We, on the other hand, have been so absorbed with the political implications in this matter that we never thought about thanking the girl. We just wanted to locate her for questioning."

Eva's gaze lowered. "I think God would be more concerned that we thank her." Her cheeks flushed slightly as all eyes turned her way. The officers looked startled, even the Chaplain.

He was the first to recover. "You sound like a woman of genuine faith," he told Eva, reaching out and touching her hand. "Perhaps I should tell you that I've informed Lt. Thornton I'm available if he ever wants to talk about spiritual matters. But for now he seems quite doubtful that God cared about him in Indochina . . . ."

Captain Wickman shuffled uneasily in his chair. "Yes, well, ah—" he began.

The Commander cleared his throat, an attention-getter he had used several times in our few hours of knowing him. "We've given you as much background as we can. Now let's have Captain Wickman brief you on Lt. Thornton's medical care."

The Captain's serious dark eyes took in the three of us, then settled on Eva. "The Commander tells us you want your son home for Christmas. Perhaps in a week we can release him—in time for the holidays."

"He'll be discharged then?" inquired Eva.

"From the hospital, but not from the Navy. That will come after he's cleared medically. In the meantime, we will continue his care on an outpatient basis. Mr. Ballard has assured the Commander that it will not be a problem for Lt. Thornton to commute to San Diego daily, Monday through Friday."

Eva and I stared at David. He looked almost sheepish. "Eva, I called the Commander last evening," he admitted, "after you two turned in. I couldn't sleep. The Commander and I chatted a bit and I told him again how much we want Rob home for Christmas. We'll get him here for treatment every day if I have to fly him in my Bonanza."

Eva broke in. "I'd like to know more about Rob's health. When will he regain his memory? What sort of treatment will he need?"

Wickman formed an arc with his fingertips. "Apart from Lt. Thornton's amnesia and his recent bout with malaria, he's in reasonably good condition. The malaria is under control. As you already suspect, our biggest concern now is his amnesia."

"But I thought the malaria caused Rob's amnesia," said Eva.

"The malaria only aggravated it. Our Cat Scan

indicates that Lt. Thornton suffered a head injury many years ago—either when his plane crashed or in the subsequent grenade explosion. With that concussion, followed by years of mental and psychological trauma from his prolonged imprisonment. . . ." He paused, allowing his words to penetrate, then went on. "The Lieutenant has blocked out a great deal. If we can help him to regain his memory, his recovery may be more rapid. For now, we've set up counseling three times a week with one of our psychiatrists—"

"A psychiatrist!" Eva protested.

The Captain's tone was placatory. "We're most likely dealing with a case of post-traumatic stress syndrome, Mrs. Thornton. We know from past experience that prisoners of war often suffer painful flashbacks and severe depression. We want to do everything possible to alleviate these symptoms in your son."

Eva sat straight, unblinking. The stoic composure that characterized her at work was taking over, masking her emotions. "You said Rob will need to be here every day?"

"He will. We plan daily physical therapy for his injured leg. There's a good bit of muscle atrophy there—that's a progressive wasting of the muscles. Malnutrition didn't help any."

"What a shame. My son was so active in sports. Swimming. Basketball. Track. Everything."

"I belong to a private athletic club in Orange County," said David. "I'll arrange membership there for Rob. They have tennis courts and their own Olympic-sized swimming pool. Rob can get a good workout there."

The Captain pursed his lips thoughtfully. "Let's

hold off on that for a few weeks. We'll give you the go-ahead as soon as the physical therapist approves."

"Agreed," said David. "Anything else we should know?"

"Eventually we'll be doing some bonding on his chipped incisors. We'll hold off awhile until his dental records catch up with him."

Eva's eyes riveted on Captain Wickman. "What about Rob's fingers, Captain? His burns."

"Lt. Thornton has good mobility in both hands. Some scarring, yes. But mobility is what counts." Wickman brushed some imaginary dust from his immaculate blue uniform, as though announcing the end of the conference. "And that, Mrs. Thornton, is all I can tell you now. I'll see the Lieutenant every Friday to check his progress."

"And if I can be of help, Mrs. Thornton," said the Commander, "please feel free to call my office. If I can't get back to you, the Officer of the Day will."

Eva smiled. "I appreciate all your efforts in my son's behalf."

There was a flicker of sympathy in Captain Wickman's face. "We want Lt. Thornton well again," he said, his dark eyes penetrating. "He represents over 2400 missing men. What we do for Lt. Thornton will be what we would do for each of those men if we had the chance."

Commander Thomas stood and walked around the desk to Eva. "If your son shares any pertinent information—even if it seems insignificant to you— we need to know." He offered his hand and walked her to the door. "Until now, the longest survival period in captivity for any of our Vietnam POW's was nine years. Your son went beyond that. As we've already pointed out, since he survived, there is reason to believe others may still be alive."

He shook hands with each of us, but he lingered with Eva. "Good luck to you, Mrs. Thornton. Please keep in touch."

As we left the Administration Building and headed back toward Rob's room, Lance Edwards broke into an energetic stride beside us. "Good afternoon, Mrs. Thornton, Miss Merrill. Did you have a pleasant conversation with the Commander?"

"No comment," I snapped, annoyed.

"Really? You were in there over an hour. Surely—"

"Are you spying on us, Mr. Edwards?"

David stepped between Lance and me. "Come on, man. How about showing a little respect for our privacy!"

"It's all right, David," soothed Eva. "Mr. Edwards is just interested in Rob, that's all."

"Interested in a story, you mean," I inserted.

"You're both right," Edwards smiled slyly. "Lt. Thornton has a blockbuster of a tale to tell—"

"You sound so sure of yourself," I said accusingly.

"I am," he retorted. "I was there in Thailand, remember? I've got my sources—and lots of suspicions. There's more to the Lieutenant than meets the eye."

"Please, Mr. Edwards," urged Eva, touching his arm, "my son isn't well. Please leave it alone for now."

"I'm sorry, I can't, Mrs. Thornton. There's a puzzle here. I can't rest until I have all the pieces."

"Don't you understand, Mr. Edwards? We're trying to salvage my son's life."

Lance Edwards tipped his cap in a farewell gesture. "I'll go for now, Mrs. Thornton, but let me warn you. You're sitting on a powder keg. When it blows, it'll take all of you with it."

CHAPTER SEVEN

True to their word, the Navy discharged Rob from the hospital two days before Christmas. He was flying home late this afternoon in David's Beechcraft Bonanza.

Eva had gone overboard, decorating the house with huge spiny-toothed boughs of holly and ivy and sprigs of mistletoe. She hung a wreath on the door, placed candles in every window, and strung miniature lights across the mantle. A hand-carved, olive-wood Nativity scene graced the baby grand piano, and a glittering ceramic tree made a festive centerpiece on the dining room table. Framing the archway were hundreds of cards from friends and strangers, wishing Rob well.

Early this morning, before leaving for San Diego to pick up Rob, David had driven up to a tree farm near Eva's cabin in the mountains and cut down a lush evergreen. The ceiling-high tree stood untrimmed by the bay window, its freshly cut wood smelling pungently of sap and pine. "I'll Be Home

for Christmas" echoed its familiar refrain on the
stereo.

"Do you think Rob will like the tree?" Eva fretted
as she set a box of ornaments beside the fireplace.

"He'll love it," I answered. "You've always said
Christmas was his favorite time of year."

"And mine—especially this year!"

"I have a feeling this will be the best Christmas
for all of us," I noted, thinking of David and the love
we shared.

"I hope Rob likes the condominium," continued
Eva worriedly. "It's so different from the home he
grew up in back in Indiana."

"But his room's the same," I reminded her.

She brightened. "Yes, I restored it to look exactly
as he left it."

"They should be here soon," I said, glancing at the
mantle clock. "Is there anything else you want me
to do?"

"Let's see. The roast is done. I just have to make
gravy and mash the potatoes."

I followed Eva over to the dining room table where
she absently straightened the silverware at Rob's
place setting—a subconscious gesture she had repeated again and again during the past two hours.

"Everything is perfect," I assured her. "No one
could have done more for her son than you've
done."

Her eyes moistened. "How many mothers get to
welcome home a child they thought was lost forever?" She blinked rapidly and turned to fold Rob's
linen napkin—again.

I didn't reply. My own emotions were riding close
to the surface. I wasn't about to weep and smear my
mascara. Besides, I knew there would be buckets

of joyful tears the minute Rob walked through the doorway.

Shortly after five we heard a noise on the porch. Eva and I dropped everything and hurried to the door just as David burst in with an ebullient, "Ho, ho, ho! Merry Christmas! Look what Santa brought!" David's face glowed with boyish animation. He stepped aside, revealing Rob silhouetted in the evening shadows. Rob seemed almost shy as he hesitated in the doorway, leaning on his cane.

"Come on in, man," said David, nudging Rob's elbow. "You're home, buddy."

Rob entered with an awkward, awestruck eagerness, limping slightly as he shuffled inside. He was wearing the corduroy slacks and brown argyle sweater David had bought him. His reversible tan jacket hung open, the collar upturned. His eyes, large and bright in his thin face, lingered on me for a moment, then flashed to Eva. She was radiant, laughing and crying at once as she reached out and enveloped him in her arms. He made a small chuckling sound as he nestled his chin against the top of her head.

"Darling, your hands are like ice," Eva cried, massaging them impulsively, her maternal instincts already taking over.

He shivered. "I can't get used to this winter weather. I haven't been warm since I left the tropics."

"If you think California is cold," said Eva, "you should be back in Fort Wayne, Indiana."

"Indiana? What's there?"

"The house you grew up in," said Eva softly.

Rob shook his head as if to clear it. "Oh, yeah. It

was a big house, wasn't it? There was a swing on the front porch—"

"That's right, Rob." Eva's voice rose with excitement. "It was your favorite spot. I used to rock you on that old oak swing when you were little. Do you remember how we used to watch the fireflies in summer?"

"Fireflies? Yes, I liked catching fireflies." Rob drew back slightly, his expression clouding. "But I didn't like the basement," he said vaguely. "It was damp and dark. It scared me. The coal made a terrible racket when it came down the chute. I couldn't get the black dust off my hands—"

Eva frowned quizzically. "Rob, we got rid of the coal furnace when you were little. The coal bin was empty. We switched to oil—"

"Really? I'm sure I remember it—a small, cold, dark place."

"I remember you used to hide there sometimes," said Eva. "No matter. Your hands are warmer now. Come, dinner is almost ready and I want you to see your new home before we eat." She gripped his arm and led him into the living room.

We all looked at Rob's face as his eyes settled on the Christmas tree. He beamed with pleasure.

"We're going to decorate it after dinner," David told him. "You get to hang the lights."

Rob lifted his cane. "It'll have to be the lower lights."

"I saved all the old decorations you made for me in school," said Eva, her voice suddenly choking with emotion. She leaned down and opened a cardboard box beside the tree, then showed him the fragile items one by one. "I took these treasures out each year but it hurt too much to hang them up.

But now! Now I want every one of them on the tree—the paper Santas, your clay handprint, the Styrofoam angel you made in third grade, the carved frame with your sixth grade picture—"

He scooped up a cotton snowman. "Did I make this, too?"

"Oh, yes. You were in first grade. You used the buttons from your dad's pajamas for the eyes. You borrowed my sewing scissors, no less. Your father was furious until you brought the snowman to him and gave him a big hug." Her eyes brimmed with tears. "That was his last Christmas with us."

Rob bent down and put the ornament back in the box. He straightened, a troubled look in his eyes. "Perhaps if we were back in Indiana," he said apologetically, "perhaps then I'd remember."

"It's all right, son. You'll remember in time."

"Did we always put up a tree—Mom?"

"Every Christmas. We never missed a one—even that winter you had a job at the post office. I waited until you got home on Christmas Eve, then we stayed up till the wee small hours hanging the trimmings."

"Mom, you really love Christmas, don't you?"

"And I love eating," teased David, eyeing the dining room table.

"Eva's not feeding us until she gives Rob the grand tour," I told him.

David pulled me close and nuzzled my neck. "Better be a quick tour or I'll forget I'm hungry." He kissed me tenderly until I pulled back in embarrassment.

"Not here, David," I whispered.

"Why not? Rob knows about us." He kissed me

again. "I talked about you all the way home from San Diego."

Rob's attention was already turned to the baby grand piano. He ran his fingers over the keyboard, then sat down and began playing "White Christmas," stiffly, woodenly at first, then with surprising dexterity.

Eva looked at Rob in amazement. "I'd forgotten you could play so well." Her gaze turned to David and me. She laughed lightly. "And to think of that ruler I broke on his bottom to get him to practice. Those piano lessons paid off after all."

She rested her hand on Rob's shoulder as he attempted another song. "You play beautifully," she repeated.

He cast us a melancholy smile. "During my years in the prison camps, I played the piano in my mind to break the tedium. All the songs I could remember, over and over."

"You remember that?" asked David.

Rob stopped in the middle of a stanza and stood up, staring at his hands. "Yes, I really did do that. I played tunes in my mind."

"It's all right, Rob. You'll have lots of time now to play. Meanwhile, let me show you your room," said Eva.

David and I followed them down the hallway. "That's mine," she said, barely pausing at the master bedroom. Then she entered the next room and motioned us inside. Rob took a sweeping glance and whistled through his teeth. "You mean all this stuff is mine?" He scanned the faded banners, the trophies, the yellowed photographs. Picking up a pair of worn sneakers still laced together over the bedpost, he half chuckled. "Didn't you throw away anything in all these years?"

"I couldn't bear to part with any of your posses-sions, darling."

He tossed the sneakers back on the bed. "At least I hope you remembered to wash the socks."

David laughed. "You don't know Eva if you think she'd allow any dirty laundry in her house."

Rob sobered immediately. "You're right. I don't know her."

"No offense, man," said David quickly. "You'll know her in time. She's been a mother to me too, you know. I kept my promise to you and looked her up after Vietnam. It's one of the best things I ever did."

Rob cuffed David good-naturedly. "I'm glad, buddy. I'm just going to need your help—and Mom's—to get it all together, okay?"

"We're all with you, Rob. You can count on us." David looked at me. "Right, Michelle?"

I stepped between the two towering men, embrac-ing them both. "I'll do anything I can to help you, Rob," I promised. Silently I was already praying that Rob would remember his past now that he was among his own things. I saw the same hope in Eva's expression as Rob broke away and tapped one of the model airplanes dangling from the ceiling. He watched it whirl around with mute fascination, then wandered around the room, scrutinizing every picture and pennant. "Purdue," he murmured wistfully. "Was that my alma mater?"

"Yes." Eva squeezed Rob's shoulder reassuringly. "It'll all come back. I know it will, son." She handed him a photograph. "Do you recognize this girl?"

He studied it intently. "She's pretty—"

"She was your steady girl. Tammy Marlor. A

lovely person. I still hear from her every Christmas. Her card's there in the archway. She's so glad you're home. She'd love to see you again."

"Maybe someday," Rob said without conviction. His eyes met mine and crinkled slightly. "She's not as pretty as you, Michelle."

I felt my face flush. "Thank you, Rob."

David slipped his arm around me. "Sorry, she's taken, old man."

Eva broke in pleasantly with, "You young people can gab all you want, but if I don't get back to the kitchen, we'll have bricks instead of mashed potatoes!"

"I'm with you," said David.

"Me too," said Rob. "I feel like I've been waiting half my life for a home-cooked meal."

The dinner turned out to be one of Eva's best. Rob ate as heartily as he could—but it was obvious that his taste buds were just coming back, that for now he could eat only sparingly. "It tastes so good," he kept saying. "You've gone to so much work. I—I just can't eat everything. Not yet."

"Oh, but just wait," said David. "Eva's made your favorite dessert—lemon meringue pie."

Eva silenced David with a frown.

Rob shrugged, half apologetically. "After a steady diet of Laotian food—rice, corn, fish sauce, and cabbage soup—my stomach just can't handle rich food yet."

"Well, you just let me know what you can eat and that's what I'll fix," Eva assured him. "Let's forget the pie for now. I'll serve coffee in the living room."

"While we're trimming the tree?" asked Rob with sudden eagerness. He pushed back his seat, stood up and removed his cane from the back rung of the chair. "Race you for the lights, Dave," he grinned, then turned and limped in a lumbering gait toward the living room. David took three strides and was beside Rob, tossing a comradely arm around his shoulder.

Eva and I exchanged pleased, teary glances. "It's a miracle, Michelle. Both my boys home for Christmas!"

CHAPTER
EIGHT

On the Saturday after Christmas, David and I took Rob shopping for clothes. We made the rounds of Brooks Brothers, The Broadway, and Essex Shoppe for Men. David helped Rob pick out stylish ties, shirts, sportswear, and even a three-piece gray suit. For casual dress, David suggested oxford button-down shirts, khaki trousers, loafers, and white socks.

Rob smiled wryly. "For casual, I'm used to baggy peasant pajamas."

"Those days are over," said David, sounding almost reprimanding.

Rob struggled with the pale blue tie that accented his three-piece suit. "I'm not sure how to do this."

David went over and expertly knotted Rob's tie. "There. How's that?"

Rob still looked uncertain. "Don't know where I'll wear this," he mumbled as the tailor measured the pant legs.

"How about church?" suggested David.

"Well, I sure won't need a three-piece suit for

work," frowned Rob. "I'll be lucky if I can scrounge up a blue collar job."

"There's plenty of time to think about work," David told him. "Right now you just need to concentrate on your therapy."

Rob bristled. "That's easy for you to say, Dave. You're a big success. Own your own company. Call all the shots. Who knows? Maybe if I'd made it out when you did, I'd be a rich man now, too!"

I looked up quickly at David, in time to catch the fleeting pain that registered for an instant and then hardened into mute anger. Did Rob have any idea how cutting his remarks were? Or how David had suffered all these years thinking he had been responsible for Rob's death?

I made it a point to keep my thoughts to myself and let the two men make their own faltering way back to each other. But first Rob would have to regain his memory. Only then could each man spill out his soul—the torment and the rage, the guilt and recriminations. Perhaps then they could truly pick up their friendship again.

My thoughts scattered as Rob said, "What do you think, Michelle?" He stood staring somberly at his reflection in the full-length, three-way mirror.

"You look very handsome," I told him sincerely. With his beard neatly trimmed and his lanky frame beginning to fill out a little, Rob was indeed a strikingly imposing man. But his was not a typical attractiveness. He possessed something more, indefinable—an ambivalent fire, a beleaguered sensitivity—almost an unarticulated rage just beneath the surface.

I wondered if anyone else saw what I saw. Most of the time a gentle, soft-spoken veneer covered

Rob's roiling emotions. I glimpsed the rage and fire only in his eyes and only during rare, unguarded moments.

Rob's expression clouded as he turned to one side, apparently scrutinizing the angles and planes of his face. "I can't get used to it," he said.

"What, Rob?"

"That. Me. How can I be sure whose face it is?" He gestured toward the mirror. "We didn't have mirrors in the prison camps or the villages. Just rivers and streams to catch our reflection. You couldn't see much—just a distorted image."

"You look fine," I began helplessly.

"The suit does, but my face—it startles me every time I see it. It's not familiar. It's old, worn." He leaned forward and ran his hand over his nose and chin. "It could be the face of someone on the street, a stranger. I could pass this face by and not even know it."

"Oh, Rob, it's a wonderful face. It has such sensitivity."

He gave me a long, penetrating gaze. "You really think so, Michelle?"

The tailor stood up and interrupted with, "Okay, young man, I've got all the measurements. You can go change now. I'll have your suit ready next Friday."

David stepped forward and removed several bills from his wallet. "What's the chance of having it ready by this evening?"

The bald little man grinned eagerly, his marble-black eyes dancing. "I'll get right on it, sir. Have it for you by five."

We left the shop and made our way through the after-Christmas crowds to a nearby restaurant in the mall for lunch. Rob was visibly perspiring as we sat down in a corner booth. "Are you okay?" I asked.

He put his head in his hands.

"Hey, man, we can go straight home if you don't feel well," said David.

Rob shook his head as if dazed. He mopped his face with his handkerchief. "So many people—the noise—confusion. It hits me—I need space—air."

I reached over and touched Rob's hand. It was icy cold. "It's okay, Rob. We'll go home. I can pick the suit up later."

Rob looked around, agitated, his eyes wide and frantic. "All these stores—there's no silence any-where—just noise—the music, its beat thundering in my head."

"The songs are all like that these days, Rob," said David, "but it's quieter here. Listen, the music's almost mellow."

"We could have something quick—maybe a cup of soup—" I said.

"Just to warm us up and take the edge off our hunger," added David. "Besides, Eva will want to feed us the minute we get home." He signaled the waitress and ordered three tureens of chicken noodle soup and three cups of hot chocolate.

By the time we finished our soup, Rob's spirits had lifted. He seemed calmer now, almost happy as he relished his cup of hot chocolate. "You know, I'd almost forgotten anything could taste so good," he sighed. There was a dot of whipped cream on his mustache. Impulsively I reached over and dabbed it with my napkin.

Rob looked amused, pleased.

When I glanced over at David he seemed mildly an-noyed. "I think we'd better go," he said impatiently.

He stood and reached for his wallet.

"Let me catch this one, Dave," Rob told him. "I have all that back pay burning in my pocket."

With Rob feeling better, we decided to browse around the mall until his suit was ready. We inched our way through the gift-exchanging throngs in the Broadway, May Company, and Computerland. I could tell that the crowds still ruffled Rob, but he was fascinated by all the new electronic gadgets and innovations. He had never seen personal computers, video cassette recorders, solar calculators, or cordless phones. He stared awestruck at a pocket-sized, three-inch color TV and shook his head in disbelief over the home satellite TV systems with their motorized 8-foot receptor-dishes.

"I feel like I've been gone a hundred years," Rob exclaimed under his breath. "Everything's so different, so fast. How do you keep up? How do you survive?"

"You get jaded after awhile," reflected David. "You see so much you lose the wonder of it all." He cuffed Rob's arm. "Come over here. You'll like video games."

"Oh, David, no," I protested. "We don't have time."

"Sure we do." He led Rob over to a counter brimming with every variety of video game—Star Wars, Demolition Derby, Pac-Man, Demon Attack, Donkey Kong. "If you ever played pinball as a kid, you'll get a kick out of these."

"I don't know," replied Rob, leaning on his cane. "I can't remember what I did as a kid." He stared at the flickering screen in puzzlement as David began to demonstrate the finer points of destroying enemy missiles on the video screen. I sighed wearily and wandered over to the furniture department.

Rob caught up with me minutes later and touched my arm.

"What's the matter? The game over already?" I asked.

"Those things are weird—the flashing lights and images—blinding—" Rob's complexion was ashen. Beads of perspiration dotted his forehead.

I realized in alarm that David and I, with our good intentions, were exhausting Rob. "Well, if we have to wait on David," I said, nodding toward the velvet European sofa on sale, "let's at least be comfortable."

"No need to sit down," David said abruptly from behind us. "Let's just go pick up Rob's suit and go home."

Before we left the store, Rob paused by a display counter of Hummel figurines and Swiss handcrafted music boxes. Carefully he picked up an exquisite, delicately painted chalet with miniature figures. He wound it and listened to the lyrical, haunting melody of "Somewhere, My Love." His eyes glistened with a faraway wistfulness.

"It's lovely," I murmured.

Rob broke from his reverie and smiled at me. "I'm going to get it for Eva. She'd like it, wouldn't she?"

"She'd adore it!"

By the time we had finished our shopping and picked up Rob's suit and his other purchases, our arms were loaded with packages. "It's Christmas all over again," I exclaimed when we entered the condominium a half hour later.

Eva emerged from the kitchen with a spatula in her hand. "Oh, good, you're just in time for dinner. Oh, and look at all the shopping you've done! If I hadn't had my hair appointment, I would have gone with you."

David and I dropped our parcels on the sofa. "We bought the town out," I said cheerily.

"And I bought this for you, Mom," said Rob, thrusting his gift awkwardly into her hands.

"For me?"

"Yeah. I thought you'd like it." He sank down in exhaustion into the cushioned chair by the tree, then leaned forward with effort on his cane as Eva tore off the wrappings. "You'd better sit down before you drop it," he cautioned.

She sat on the edge of the nearest chair and gently lifted the chalet from the box. "It's beautiful, Rob!"

"Like you," he said shyly.

She wound the music box and placed it gently on the piano. "Thank you, son. I'll treasure it always."

"So what's been happening around here?" asked David.

"Captain Wickman called while you were out."

Rob's eyes narrowed. "I'm not going back to the hospital."

"You don't have to, darling, not until after the holidays."

"And then you'll just be an outpatient," David reminded him.

"The Captain just wanted to know how you were," continued Eva. She picked up the newspaper and handed it to Rob. "Son, I thought you might want to take a look at this article by Lance Edwards."

At the mention of Edwards, I leaned over Rob's shoulder and stared at the black headlines: POW ROB THORNTON HOME FOR HOLIDAYS.

"That infuriating man never gives up," I exclaimed.

"I don't think he means any harm, Michelle," said Eva.

I didn't reply, but in my opinion there was nothing harmless about Lance Edwards. Skimming the article, I was more convinced than ever when I read his closing sentence: "Thornton refuses to talk with the press about his elusive, forgotten years in Indochina, which raises the probing question, *What is the Lieutenant trying to hide?*"

CHAPTER NINE

By the second Friday in January, David insisted we spend an evening alone. Early that morning, shortly after Eva and Rob left for their seventh trip to the Naval Hospital, he telephoned. "Michelle, I've made reservations for a dinner show this evening. Bring a change of clothes to work—we'll leave directly from there."

"Sounds wonderful." I didn't tell David, but I would be glad to be free for a while from the mounting tensions in the Thornton household. "What's playing?" I asked.

"Cole Porter's *Kiss Me Kate*."

"Isn't that the musical version of *The Taming of the Shrew*?"

"Right. I thought an old Shakespeare fan like you would enjoy it."

At work that morning David passed me two or three times, gave an expectant wink, acknowledged Mitzi Piltz as she gave him a fluttery wave, then hurried on to his office. He had appointments all afternoon but promised to be finished in time for our date. "Be ready by five-thirty," he told me.

In spite of the heavy weekend traffic, David was relaxed as we drove from Irvine to the Sebastian Playhouse in San Clemente. Even during dinner, he kept the conversation light, carefully avoiding any mention of Rob and Eva. I was certain that David had noticed the subtle changes in Eva. She was becoming increasingly subdued, almost depressed over the wild mood swings in Rob since he had begun his outpatient treatments in San Diego. He was particularly disoriented and angry, his emotions almost ungovernable, on those days when he had his counseling sessions with the psychiatrist. This would be one of those days.

"Come back to me," David was saying. "This is our evening together." We were sitting at a small table for two, waiting for the curtain to rise.

"I'm sorry," I murmured. "My thoughts were wandering."

"Not far, I hope."

"Never far from you, David," I promised dreamily.

As David sipped his after-dinner coffee, I absently straightened the gold chain on my diamond pendant—David's Christmas gift to me. He watched me intently, finally nodding at the necklace. "You were disappointed, weren't you?"

"Disappointed?"

"Your necklace."

I could feel my cheeks flush, but I prayed that David wouldn't notice.

"Well?" he pressed.

"It's beautiful, David—and much too expensive."

"But you expected a diamond ring?"

I fought sudden tears, remembering guiltily how disappointed I had been on Christmas morning when I opened the tiny package. Even this one-carat diamond solitaire didn't have the significance of a modest engagement ring. "I just thought—," I stammered.

As if reading my thoughts, David assured me, "There will be a ring, Michelle. But nothing's been normal lately. I want a ring to be special—not crowded into these recent tumultuous weeks."

The theatre lights flickered. Five minutes before curtain time.

"The ring will match your necklace," David persisted, taking my hand. "Trust me, Michelle. It didn't seem right to give ourselves that exclusive, joyful moment when Rob is struggling so desperately to belong. I just couldn't exclude him from anything during the holidays. And now . . ."

"Things aren't much better, are they? I guess we all expected too much, too soon."

David nodded. "I had hoped that Rob would improve rapidly once he got some psychiatric help at the hospital. But it seems he's only getting worse, retreating more into himself all the time."

"I know what you mean," I said somberly. "David, Rob is up prowling around in his room, night after night. I don't know when he sleeps."

"He looks like he never sleeps," declared David. "His face is drawn, his eyes glazed. Sometimes he's so detached."

"It's like he's trying to insulate himself from the whole world."

"He's just not the same friendly, outgoing guy I knew in Vietnam."

"Did you expect him to be?"

"I don't know what I expected." David paused, scrutinizing me. "I hope you aren't losing any sleep over this whole thing, Michelle."

"Actually, I did last night. Rob's bed is on the other side of my bedroom wall. In the middle of the night, I was awakened by several violent thuds. He must have been hitting the wall."

"In his sleep?"

"I don't know. I heard him cry out. It was a piercing, tormented shriek. It must have been a nightmare. I know from experience how terrifying they can be."

"That's right. You haven't mentioned your nightmares lately."

"I haven't had them since moving in with Eva."

David gave me a quizzical glance. "When Rob called out—what did you do? Did you go to him?"

I met David's gaze. "By the time I put on my robe and went down the hall to his room, it was quiet again. But Eva was awake."

"Did you talk to her?"

"No, I didn't," I replied as the Playhouse lights dimmed. "I listened outside her door. Eva was crying—and praying, I think."

"Praying for her son," David noted.

"Aren't we all!" I replied.

Darkness engulfed us as the Cole Porter lyrics liltingly filled the room and the curtains opened on *Kiss Me Kate*. But I almost missed the opening lines of the play as my thoughts remained on Eva's growing concern for Rob. In a counterpoint of memory I recalled her great joy as she introduced her son to the church congregation the Sunday before last. What pride! What joy! Gratitude radiated in her face and voice. Then I pictured Rob's restlessness as he squirmed in the pew, looking ill at ease in his new gray suit. Moments later, in the middle of the sermon, he suddenly got up and walked out of the service.

My disquieting memories of Rob evaporated as David slipped his arm around my shoulder, drawing me back to the lively antics of the characters on stage. I nestled against him and turned my attention to the play, resolving to put everything else out of my mind.

I'm glad I did. *Kiss Me Kate* was delightful. David and I found ourselves laughing, humming, and tapping our feet to the music. During the romantic scenes, he squeezed my hand, a mischievous smile on his lips.

We left the theatre well after midnight and walked arm in arm to David's Mercedes, giddy as frolicking children. Minutes later, when we entered the freeway onramp, David turned south on Freeway 405. "I thought we were going home, David," I said, glancing around.

"We are—the long way. I know a quaint, little spot near Oceanside. The beach is superb, the view incredible. I want you to see it."

"I'd love to," I sighed, settling back contentedly.

"Anything to be together a little longer—at last," he teased gently, pulling me close. "I hardly see you anymore without Eva or Rob around."

"I know. Sometimes it's infuriating. But at least we have tonight. I'm just glad we don't work tomorrow."

He chuckled. "Who knows? We may not find our way home until Monday."

"Oh, David!" I chided.

Shortly he pulled off the road near a sandy cove

and parked. For a while we sat in a casual embrace listening to the ardent refrains of a romantic ballad on the car stereo. We watched the powerful, rhythmic ballet of crashing ocean meeting windswept beach. A pale winter moon hung in the star-spangled sky, its silver rays spinning us in a crystal cocoon of enchantment.

"It's a perfect night," David whispered against my ear. His breath was warm, his voice caressing. The moist sea air was already seeping into my bones, making me shiver. David's mouth moved against my cheek. "I love you, Michelle." He drew me closer, crushing me in his arms. We kissed until I forgot the music and the chill. Time dissolved. His kisses grew more urgent. My emotions were pinwheeling, riding the edge of ecstasy.

Then David broke away with an abruptness that startled me. "Michelle, Michelle," he uttered with a riveting torment, "what you do to me!"

Our gaze locked. His face was a silhouette of shadows and moonlight. I melted in his eyes. "What are we going to do, David?"

He straightened and reached for his keys. "I think this is one of those times when the only way to win the battle is to run."

"I'm glad you're strong," I admitted. I was trembling.

"Strong nothing," David said huskily. "I'm just smart enough to know how weak I am."

Neither of us said much during the drive home. I kept thinking how hard it was to let David go, to continue facing the long nights alone. I wanted David. I yearned for marriage, for the freedom to give our love full expression. Could we wait until spring, as my father asked? Was it foolish and punishing even to try? Could God give us the strength to remain pure? He had so far, but tonight we had come close to testing the limits. It would have been so easy to step over. What would happen next time?

When David finally pulled into the parking space beside Eva's condominium, he looked over and said contritely, "I'm sorry, Michelle."

"Sorry?"

He cleared his throat uneasily. "I almost crossed over the line between love and exploitation tonight. I apologize."

"You aren't any more guilty than I am," I stammered. I didn't admit it aloud, but I had felt keenly disappointed when David turned away so suddenly.

"We've got to make some decisions, Michelle," he went on in his tight, practical tone. "Either we move up our wedding date or we cool it a little."

"You mean not see each other?"

"No—just avoid the lonely beaches and empty apartments, that sort of thing—"

The words caught in my throat. "No more cuddling?"

"It might be cuddling to you, Michelle, but—frankly, I'm not made of ice or steel. I'm only human, and I've waited a long time. You're making it awfully difficult to wait much longer."

"Waiting isn't easy for me either," I confessed, my voice wavering slightly. "But I—I want us to have a relationship that pleases the Lord."

"That's what I want too. We've got so much going for us, Michelle, I don't want to spoil it now." David took both my hands in his. "Do you realize how special it is that we both still have that precious gift to give each other? I want us to be able to give it with God's blessing, as husband and wife."

It was after two a.m. when we got out of the car. David walked me to the door. The lights were still on inside. "Someone must be waiting up for you," he said.

I quickly unlocked the door. "I hope there's no problem."

David followed me inside. Eva was up, wrapped snugly in her rose velvet robe, curled comfortably in the rocker in the living room, reading her Bible. "I thought you two would never get home," she said with a knowing smile. "But I'm glad you had an evening out together."

"How'd it go today, Eva?" David asked, pocketing his car keys.

She glanced hastily down the hallway toward the bedrooms before answering. "Stressful. Rob saw Captain Wickman this morning. That went fairly well. But when he came out of Dr. Foster's office—"

"The psychiatrist?" I asked.

Eva nodded. "Rob looked like he'd been crying. He didn't say a word all the way home." She sighed. "He hardly touched his dinner. He's been in his room all evening."

"It's rough on you, Eva," said David.

"And rough on Rob," she answered tremulously.

"Has Rob opened up at all?"

"Not really. I thought the trips down to San Diego would be good for us, for both of us. I wanted that time alone with Rob to talk about the past, to help him remember. We were so close before—so many years ago. I wanted to recapture a little bit of that." Tears welled in her eyes. "But I don't seem to say anything right."

"What do you mean?" David asked.

"The more I say, the more I antagonize Rob." She was crying now. "Captain Wickman says I'm pushing him too hard—he says Rob doesn't want to remember."

"That's crazy, Eva," David shot back. "Why wouldn't Rob want to remember?"

"The Captain says he's afraid of opening up to me." Eva wrung her hands, distraught. "Imagine, David—Rob afraid of his own mother!"

"He's not afraid of you, Eva," I declared. "He's afraid of himself, afraid to let go of this Cory Rugby, the only identity he knows. He's trying so hard to please us, to be Rob Thornton."

David looked thoughtful. "You know, maybe Rob needs a change of scene. In fact, maybe we could all use a change. What about a weekend at your cabin, Eva? The mountain air would do us all good."

"You mean all four of us?" asked Eva.

"Sure. Why not?"

"I'm game," I told David eagerly. "Eva's been promising to take me up to see the snow. She tells me it's a writer's paradise."

"Then how about if I drive us up next weekend?" suggested David.

Eva stood up and set her Bible on the coffee table. "You're so good to me, David." She came over and kissed us both good night, then turned to go to her room. She hesitated, pivoted and managed a faint smile. "There was one good thing about today's visit. I ran into Commander Thomas while Rob was at physical therapy. We had lunch together. He's a most charming man."

"Married?" I questioned slyly.

There was a twinkle in Eva's eyes. "No. He's a widower."

CHAPTER
TEN

After church on Sunday morning, the weather was still cool, a brisk wind whipping around the corners of the building as I made my way out to the parking lot. As usual David was spending a few extra minutes with his class of junior highers, being their friend, answering their questions, experiencing that special camaraderie he had with his boys. Eva had already driven Rob home between services. He had grown restless, on edge again, twisting his bulletin into a jagged propeller.

Even before I could slip into the passenger seat of David's Mercedes, I spotted Lance Edwards striding toward me. I wondered if Eva had gone home just because of Rob or for fear of another encounter with that obnoxious reporter. Edwards reached the car before I could shut the door and leaned down with his audacious grin. "Good morning, Miss Merrill. You certainly are an early bird today."

"You know the old saying," I quipped dryly. "The

early bird gets the worm...and I've just encountered mine."

"Oh, what bitter words after such a fine sermon on loving your neighbor, Miss Merrill. And I am your neighbor, you know."

"Really? Somehow I pictured you as more the Prodigal than my neighbor."

"That too," he said, his smile vanishing.

I felt suddenly guilty. Why, oh why, did Lance Edwards bring out the worst in me? I should have been welcoming him to our church. After all, he may have come honestly seeking help. Just as I was about to say something to smooth over our dissension, Lance spoke up and shattered my momentary penitence.

"Your friend Rob Thornton seemed awfully jittery in church. What's his problem—a guilty conscience?"

"Certainly not," I said icily, "but I'm surprised your conscience isn't bothering you, Mr. Edwards. You haven't stopped annoying us since Rob came home."

"I have a job to do, Miss Merrill."

"Not a hatchet job!"

"Don't fault me for hacking away at the facts. Everyone deserves to know the truth."

"What truth?" I shot back. "Just what is it you expect to find?"

Edwards' eyes narrowed malevolently. "The connection between Rob Thornton and the man he claims to be. Are you really convinced, Miss Merrill, that Lt. Thornton is suffering memory loss? Or is he hiding behind the balm of amnesia to keep from facing what really happened in Southeast Asia?" His voice sliced the air with sarcasm. "What

I want to know is how Rob Thornton escaped and Cory Rugby got left behind."

My breath caught in my throat. I realized with a sinking sensation that Edwards wasn't just a newsman grinding out a story; this man had a personal vendetta, a score of his own to settle. "What do you know about Cory Rugby?" I asked warily.

Edwards' face was blotched with anger; the vein in his neck throbbed as he straightened and squared his shoulders. "I was in Thailand when the story blew, remember?"

I tried for a little civility in my voice. "I remember, but I don't recall exactly why you were there."

He hesitated, weighing his words. "I was doing a story on Vietnam Vets."

"You mean MIA's?"

"Not this time. I was writing about the vets who've settled in Thailand rather than returning to the States. They're an aimless bunch living in the past, still caught up in the mystique of the war."

"But what about that article you showed me the first time you came to the house—about tracking MIA's?"

"I'd hoped to do that too—get in on a search team into Laos or Vietnam to check out our downed aircraft. Mercy missions, they call them." His anger was back, not in his face but in his words. "The officer in charge didn't want a freelance reporter tagging along."

"It's noble of you to write about MIA's, but I don't understand why you're so determined to persecute Rob Thornton."

"If he turns out to be a phony—and I think that's a distinct possibility—I wouldn't want him to besmirch the name of our MIA's and POW's."

"That's ridiculous, Mr. Edwards. You have no evidence to suggest that Rob is trying to deceive anyone."

He shrugged. "It's a reporter's job to pose questions and seek answers."

"You've got the wrong questions and obviously the wrong answers!" I tried again to pull the car door shut. From the corner of my eye I saw David cutting across the parking lot toward us. Smugly I said, "You'd better go. Mr. Ballard won't like finding you here."

"Two questions first," he said, holding the door fast. "Ask your lieutenant—did he side with the enemy to gain his freedom? More importantly, what foul play befell the real Cory Rugby?" Before I could offer a comeback, he slammed the door shut, wheeled around, and stalked away.

Moments later David climbed into the driver's seat and kissed me on the cheek. "Trouble again with Lance Edwards?"

"Don't even ask," I muttered.

"I see he didn't wait to greet me."

I sighed in exasperation. "He doesn't pick on anyone his own size."

As David swung his car out of the parking lot, he said, "After your encounter with Edwards, you're probably in no mood to discuss a new job."

"New job? Are you firing me?"

"No, just reassigning you."

"What do you mean?"

"I need Eva back at the office. The work is piling up. She's the expert on contracts and negotiations."

"Where do I fit in?" I asked cautiously.

"Would you consider chauffeuring?"

"Rob?"

"Right."

"You mean drive him every day to San Diego? I don't think Eva would go for it."

"I'll persuade her. She's under too much stress, Michelle. She's too emotionally spent to handle the daily trips. Besides, the psychiatrist thinks she's putting undue pressure on Rob. I think she needs a change of scene, and you know yourself, work at the office is a sure cure for her."

"It may be a change of scene for Eva, David, but it means you and I won't see each other every day."

"It won't be forever, Michelle. And we can always spend the evenings together."

"Who will do my work at the office?" I asked, stifling my disappointment.

"Mitzi Piltz has offered to work overtime."

"Not with you, I hope!"

David laughed. "Really, Michelle, you've misjudged the lady. She's really very earnest. She genuinely wants to help Eva."

"Are you saying I don't?" I asked in a small, abashed voice.

"Of course not! That's why I knew you'd be glad to go along with my idea. You're not emotionally involved with Rob like Eva and I are. You can be objective, detached. Maybe Rob won't feel so threatened by you. In fact, I'm hoping he'll open up and share some of his hurts. Until he does, we'll never find the old Rob."

I gave David a probing glance. "Have you and Eva considered that the old Rob may be gone forever? Maybe you need to accept the man who came home and go on from there."

David's jaw clenched. "The man I knew is there, somewhere. I'll reach him if it's the last thing I do."

"For whom, David? For yourself or for Rob?"

The car swerved slightly as he stared at me. "What's that supposed to mean?"

"You can never go back to the day the plane crashed, David. You can never rescue the man Rob was twelve years ago."

David spoke over a profound sorrow. "Then I'll rescue the man who's here now." After a moment his tone grew perfunctory. "You didn't answer me. Will you make the daily drives to San Diego?"

I tried for a little lightness. "Does this mean a pay raise?"

"How about a gas allowance?"

"Sold," I said with more conviction than I felt. "By the way, do Eva and Rob know about this new arrangement?"

"I'll tell them this afternoon."

"There's just one fly in the ointment, David. My kid sister Pam is flying in Tuesday morning for a visit."

He gave me a startled glance. "So she's actually coming?"

"I didn't know for sure until she telephoned last night. The hospital where she got her nurses' training offered her a night shift, but she's bored with the dull routine of the old hometown."

David chuckled. "Well, it's anything but dull around here."

"I told Pam it was poor timing, but she said she'd like to try a little sun and surf."

"And check out the men, I bet."

"Yeah, that's Pam. She's ready to spread her wings. She'd love to get out from under Mom and Dad's thumb. But I imagine she's also planning to check you out for my dad."

"Then I'd better be on my best behavior."

"I just realized, I won't be able to meet her plane if I'm in San Diego."

"Don't worry. I'll pick Pam up. Anything for dear old Dad. Besides, she might be just what the doctor ordered for Rob."

"That's what Eva said when I asked if Pam could stay a few days."

Pam was already at the house when Rob and I arrived home from the San Diego Naval Hospital on Tuesday night. I could hear her hearty, husky laughter as we entered the door. We found David and Pam in the kitchen, standing cozily beside the stove. She was feeding him a medallion of sauteed veal. For a moment they didn't even see us.

In a single glance, I saw Pam's tilted head, her beckoning pouty smile so fresh and childlike, and her striking blue-gray eyes gazing provocatively at David. She was even more lovely than I remembered. Her long, tawny hair with flecks of burnished gold was piled high on her head and flowed in natural ringlets down her back.

"Hello, Pam," I said tightly. "I see you've made yourself at home."

She looked over in surprise, her face lighting with animation, and broke away from David. Enveloping me in a hug, she gushed, "Oh, Michelle, you should have been here today. We've had a simply marvelous time! We drove the long way home so I could see the ocean. It's terrific. I may never go back to Illinois." She gasped for breath and went on, "Look, I fixed David my special recipe— sauteed veal with Madeira sauce. I insisted he let me repay him for all his trouble, picking me up at the airport and all."

She released me and turned to Rob. "You're Rob, David's friend. Goodness, you are a good-looking man."

Before Rob could utter a word, she embraced him too. He looked startled but pleased.

David came over and gave me a hug. "Hey, Michelle, you didn't tell me what a charmer your sister is."

Through clenched teeth I said, "I knew you'd find out soon enough."

Pam broke in again. "This house is awesome, Michelle. And our bedroom—it's gorgeous. I borrowed a few of the dresser drawers. I put some of your stuff in the suitcase in the closet. Hope you don't mind."

"Mind? I—I—"

"Of course she doesn't mind," David assured her.

"Where's Eva?" I asked.

"Working late. She should be home anytime. That's why Pam went ahead with dinner. She's a great little cook, Michelle."

I glanced around at the culinary clutter—dirty pots and pans piled high, spices scattered on the counter top, greasy water in the sink. "I hope you're better at cleaning up messes than you were when we were kids, Pam."

She grinned mischievously. "Like always, I cook, you clean."

"Great," said David. "We'll let you plan the menu for this weekend."

"What's up?" asked Pam.

"A trip to the mountains. We'll all drive up Friday evening and come back Sunday."

"You mean we're going to frolic in those gorgeous snow-capped hills?" She pretended to mold a snowball and throw it at Rob. "How about it, guys? I challenge you to an old-fashioned snowball fight."

Rob meandered over to the table and picked up an apple. He bit into it with vigor. "I'll take you on," he said. "I was the snowball champ when I was a kid."

David and I looked sharply at each other, then at Rob. His expression was puzzled. "I was the champ. I know it's true, but I don't know how I know."

Pam clasped Rob's arm encouragingly. "I bet that snowball fight will be the best thing ever—you know, doing familiar things you used to do." She grinned up at him. "Just ask me. Nurses are authorities on all subjects." She chuckled. "Now come on, Robert Thornton. Let's set the table so we can serve dinner the minute your mom gets home."

That night as we climbed into bed, Pam was still exuberant. "No wonder you like it here, Michelle— all this elegance and grandeur. I already love living in this—this lap of luxury."

I turned my face to the wall and yanked the covers up around my shoulders. *To say nothing of liking the men in the house*, I thought darkly.

CHAPTER
ELEVEN

There was no way I could persuade Pam to join Rob and me on our daily treks to San Diego. She had too many goals in mind—planning the menu for our weekend trip, checking out Ballard Computer Design Corporation, and scouting around Orange County for nursing positions.

It wasn't long before I began to think Pam intended more than a brief visit. Then, when I found her filling out job applications, I knew Pam—my sweet, shrewd goofball of a kid sister—intended to be a permanent fixture.

When Rob and I arrived home from San Diego on Friday afternoon, Pam already had our belongings packed and a basket brimming with food. With a hapless greeting, I went to my room and stretched out on the bed, too tired to think about another trip today. But Pam, who had enough energy for both of us, wasn't about to let me rest. "David will be here in an hour, so hurry, Michelle, get changed!" she exclaimed. She went over to her side of the bed and slipped a small medical kit and arm sling into her overnight case.

"Doesn't look like you have much faith in us," I quipped, glancing at the sling.

"Sure I do. I just like to be prepared—especially after what David said about Rob's condition."

"A sling won't do his emotional state much good, Pam."

"Don't worry. I'm a self-proclaimed psychiatrist to boot."

I bristled at Pam's flippant self-assurance. "You don't even know Rob. You have no idea of the enormity of his problems."

"Don't get touchy," chided Pam. "Besides, I suppose you have all the answers, big sister. You always did when we were kids."

"That's not true. Besides, you were the one who always did everything you could to please Dad."

"Not anymore. I got a touch of freedom in nursing school and I'm not about to let it go."

"So that's why you're filling out job applications. You have no intention of going back home."

Pam smiled slyly. "Not if I can help it."

We heard voices from the living room—David and Eva home already. I jumped up and grabbed my wool slacks and rust-colored pullover sweater. "Did you see my new brown ski jacket?" I asked.

"Sure, Michelle. Hope you don't mind. I plan to wear it."

"What am I supposed to wear?"

"The navy one in your closet," she replied as she snatched up her suitcase and sashayed out.

"That's my old one!" I called after her, but she was already greeting David and Eva in her buoyant, bubbly voice.

I had lost out on my new ski jacket, but I made it a point to sit in the front seat of the Mercedes beside David. Within the hour, as we drove past Riverside toward the San Bernardino Mountains, Pam seemed content in the backseat talking nonstop to Rob. By the time we turned on Waterman and made our way up the winding road toward Lake Arrowhead, we were enveloped in a murky darkness. Only the steady stream of headlights served as beacons in the blackness. The pale sheaves of light ricocheted off the mounds of snow on the road's shoulder and made eerie reflections on the metal guard rails, reminding me of the sheer drop-off a few feet away. "I'm glad you're driving and not me," I told David. "I can't see a thing. I just know we're climbing."

"I wish we were making this trip in the daylight," said Eva from the backseat. "It's absolutely gorgeous, Michelle."

"One thing about driving in the mountains," remarked David. "If a fog cover comes in, turn around and scram. It's like driving through whipped cream."

"No visibility at all?"

"Barely. But the winter snows turn this place into a ski buff's paradise." David gave me a friendly nudge. "One of these days, Michelle, I'm going to bring you up here and teach you to ski."

"I'm afraid I'd do my skiing on my posterior," I bantered.

"Oh, David, I'd love to learn how to ski," Pam spoke up eagerly.

"Well, sure, why not? One of these days I'll teach you both."

"How about you, Rob?" Pam prompted. "Want to join us?"

"Maybe one of these days, as soon as I toss out this cane."

At last, just as the endless mountain curves were rollercoasting through my stomach, we passed through the quaint alpine village of Blue Jay and finally arrived at Eva's Lake Arrowhead retreat—a charming Swiss chalet tucked among the evergreens on a lonely slope overlooking the lake.

The cottage was as tastefully decorated as Eva's condominium—with hardwood floors and hand-braided throw rugs, rustic overstuffed sofas and bulky oak tables. The rooms exuded a sweet, musky fragrance. The walls were richly paneled and studded with bookshelves. A massive stone fireplace occupied one end of the huge living room. Over the mantle hung a gleaming antique saber.

"That belonged to my great, great-grandfather," said Eva when she noticed me studying the heavy, curved, single-edged sword. "He rode with the cavalry—a fine horseman, my grandmother used to say."

"Then we came from a military family," noted Rob reflectively.

"No, son, ... although we've always had someone in the wars."

"I was sure—I thought for a minute—"

"Come on, Rob," said David. "Let's get a fire started and take the chill off this place while the girls get our supper."

"Everything's under control, guys," Pam announced. "I'll just warm up the stew and dump-lings and toss the salad. We've even got fresh apple pie."

While Eva and Pam busied themselves in the kitchen, I lingered near the fireplace, watching David and Rob coax the reluctant tendrils of fire. Wispy, curling fingers of smoke escaped in the flickering light. Then, with a crackling burst, the flames leaped hungrily around the pine-scented logs. Instinctively Rob reared back on his heels, his face contorted with a lightning flash of terror. The expression was gone immediately, but a desultory grimace remained. He stood abruptly, pivoted and, with his customary limp, walked to the bay window and stared out at the radiant wash of lights across the lake.

David went over and put a firm hand on Rob's shoulder. "What is it, man—the crash—the explosion?"

"Yes. I saw it—a colossal, white-hot ball of fire—shooting me in the air like a cannon—"

"Do you remember us crashing?" urged David cautiously.

"No, it—it's gone now."

"Are you okay?"

"Yeah, sure, fine." His voice wavered. "Thanks, Dave."

Pam emerged from the kitchen sporting a large, wooden ladle. "Stew's on," she trilled. "Last one to the kitchen does K.P."

Later, exhausted and pleasantly stuffed with beef stew and apple pie, we retired early under fluffy eiderdown quilts in the three rooms upstairs. David and Rob shared the masculine den with its matching convertible sofas. Eva took the petite sitting room while Pam and I bunked together in the large master bedroom. We left the curtains wide open so that we could watch the snowflakes swirl against the windowpanes and blanket the cedar and fir trees with a fresh luminous coat.

We woke early Saturday morning, the bright sun almost blinding through the prisms of ice on the glass. I raced Pam to the window, my bare feet rebelling against the cold hardwood floor. The world outside was a frosty phantasmagoria of ice and snow. Feathery branches swayed with glittery white. Crystalline icicles hung from the eaves like jeweled stalactites. Snowdrifts hugged the distant picturesque alpine village, cloaking its red rooftops in dazzling pearl. Surrounded by cloud-capped mountains, Lake Arrowhead glistened with a silvery, resplendent sheen, reflecting elusive air castles, a will-o'-the-wisp fairyland.

"Come on," coaxed Pam. "Let's not just admire the view. Let's go out and play!"

After breakfast, with a little effort, we persuaded Rob to join us outside. "We can't make a snowman by ourselves," Pam said petulantly. "We need a couple of able-bodied men."

"You've got David," Rob parried. "Besides, after living in Southeast Asia so many years, my bones can't tolerate these wintery winds."

Pam clasped his arm amiably. "We'll bundle you up well. Then we'll have so much fun, you'll forget all about the cold."

"I doubt it," he sighed, but he was already reaching for his fur-lined jacket.

We all pulled on our coats and boots and tied scarves around our necks. Then, with a quick wave to Eva who promised to watch from the window, we dashed outside like rollicking, mirthful youngsters.

David and I built one snowman, Rob and Pam,

another. It was good packing snow, not powdery, with just enough wetness to make it solid, malleable. We slipped and slid as we rolled the huge glistening balls toward opposite sides of the porch, leaving wide, snowless trails in our wake. We broke off evergreen twigs for arms, used pinecones for the ears, a carrot for the nose, and charred embers for eyes. Pam wrapped her wool scarf around their three-tiered snowman, then tucked Rob's cane into the molded arm.

"Hey, I need that," he protested.

"You won't much longer. You're almost as good as new."

"How would you know?" he laughed edgily.

"Look at you! You're a different person since we came to the mountains."

"I've been a different person since I got back to the States," he shot back. "But nobody will listen."

"I like you just the way you are, Robert Thornton," Pam smiled.

"Yeah?" His eyes glinted with merriment. "I like you too. In fact, you make a perfect target." He scooped up a snowball and squashed it on top of her wind-tossed hair.

"The war's on," Pam exclaimed, stooping down and shaping her own icy weapon. "Come on, David, I need reinforcements!"

"Then I get Michelle!" Rob countered. He ducked behind his snowman fortress and began forming his own crystal armory.

I sprang over beside him just as David pelted me with snow. The battle raged, nature's missiles hurtling through the air, bombarding, peppering us. The snowmen took some of the blows but we couldn't always duck in time. Pam was screaming with delight while David hollered, "Attack, charge!"

David and Pam stalked us, their arms laden with freshly made ammunition, but Rob was quick to return fire. He moved with a smooth agility, darting back and forth behind cover, striking artfully. "We're winning, Michelle," he exulted as Pam and David retreated momentarily.

But David and Pam came on with a fresh onslaught, their piercing shouts cracking the frozen air. "We gotcha cornered!" David thundered victoriously.

He and Pam scaled our snow fortress, striking at close range, buffeting us with a blizzard of snowballs. Rob recoiled, crouching on the ground. "Stop! Stop!" he begged. "I don't know anything!"

For a moment I thought he was joking. But he covered his face, cowering, his whole body trembling as he cried out, "Please don't beat me. Don't beat me again!" His words, muffled against his snow-soaked jacket, erupted in a staccato outburst: "Sir!...Rugby!...Cory Alan...Captain...U.S. Marine Corps..."

David brushed the snow from his gloved hands and bent to help Rob to his feet. "It's okay, buddy. Everything's okay," he soothed.

Rob cringed against his touch. "Don't hurt me," he whimpered.

David's tone was grave, contained. "It's all right, Lt. Thornton. The enemy is gone. You're with friends."

"No, they're dead, all dead," Rob uttered inconsolably. "You want me dead too!"

David motioned Pam and me back, then took Rob's arm. More forcefully, he said, "It's me—Dave.

Captain Ballard. You're safe, Lieutenant."

Rob straightened slowly, his face twisting with a raw torment, his eyes glazed with a hard, haunted agony. His beard was snow-flecked, his hair dripping in spidery tendrils. I wanted to reach out and touch him, comfort him. Instead, I pulled his cane loose from the battered snowman and handed it to him.

He took it dazedly, his expression momentarily slack, vacant, detached, lost in his own private reverie. But when he saw Eva standing paralyzed with fear in the open doorway, he stopped dead in his tracks. "What are you looking at?" he shrilled. "Why are you staring at me that way?"

Seized by a sudden, unreasoning fury, he broke free from David's grip, his face flushing, animated again. Regarding us with stark black eyes vibrant with betrayal, he waved his cane furiously and barked, "I'm okay, do you hear? Just leave me alone! Let me be!" He climbed the porch steps, stomping the snow from his boots, and pushed past Eva into the house.

CHAPTER TWELVE

The events of our Lake Arrowhead weekend remained unsettlingly in all our minds for weeks afterward. Although each of us was careful to speak only of our more pleasant moments in the mountains, reminiscing with a forced, guarded cheerfulness, uppermost in our thoughts was Rob's volatile, unprecedented reaction to the snowball fight.

Privately, David reminded us that this incident must have been prompted by one of those flashbacks Captain Wickman had warned us about. Pam knew about such things, she said, and had even studied similar aberrations in nurses' training. Such episodes were almost commonplace among soldiers—more so among former prisoners of war.

Rob's psychiatrist also tried to allay our fears: flashbacks were to be expected, he assured us; more would likely come. In fact, they weren't necessarily undesirable. One day a flashback might offer the key to unlocking Rob's memory.

Following our Lake Arrowhead weekend, the

Thornton household faced mounting crosscurrents of tension. Rob was uptight, increasingly withdrawn around Eva and David. Pam's perky, effervescent nature had intrigued and amused Rob at first, but now he seemed to regard her with a kind of vague neutrality. For the most part he simply ignored her or mildly tolerated her attempts to practice her nursing skills on him.

In a strange, unfathomable way, it was almost as if the snowball fight had taken on a subtle, symbolic importance of its own. Invisible, inexplicable battle lines had been drawn between us: Rob and I against Eva, Pam, and David. Because I was the only one driving Rob to San Diego, I shared his identity crisis on a daily basis, commiserating, sympathizing, groping with him for even the most insignificant clues to his personality, his past.

Rob and I established a rather convivial relationship during our daily drives to the Naval Hospital. At first our conversation remained on safe topics— the weather, the scenery, casual chitchat about the lastest TV newscasts—what the President had to say about the recent peace talks or how the economy was doing.

Gradually we talked about family matters, like Pam settling in, temporarily taking my place at the office. It had been David's idea—as usual.

"You know, David has an annoying little habit of making decisions for other people," Rob chuckled. It was already February. We were making our regular Monday morning trip to the Naval Hospital.

"Still, it was a good idea," I returned. "It frees me to drive you to San Diego, and it gives David the help he needs at the office." I didn't add, if it was such a good idea, why did I feel so uneasy about it now?

"Are you worried about Pam getting interested in David?" queried Rob, as if reading my thoughts.

My voice crackled defensively. "No. Why do you ask?"

"You seem a little reserved when the two of them talk about work together."

"I feel left out sometimes—especially with Pam being so fascinated by scientific things. She's always been so much sharper than I in math and chemistry —and now computers." I could hear envy in my tone and felt somehow relieved to be sharing my misgivings with Rob.

"You have other qualities that Pam lacks."

"Maybe," I answered, wondering whether a penchant for writing outweighed Pam's scientific skills. "But the truth is, Rob, Pam sees more of David lately than I do."

"You don't have to worry, Michelle. Pam's got her eye on that reporter Lance Edwards, not David."

"Oh, that's just Pam—she enjoys harmless flirtations with every eligible bachelor." *And why not? I reflected silently. She's never been hurt the way I was once.*

"It's more serious than that," insisted Rob. "Eva says Pam and Lance have been out together several times."

"What do you mean—dating? That's impossible! Pam knows what I think of Lance Edwards."

"That's why she hasn't mentioned her dates to you."

"You're not joking, Rob? You really mean my kid sister has been dating that man?"

He shrugged. "I didn't think it would be a declaration of war."

"It can mean only one thing," I shot back impulsively. "Lance Edwards is using Pam. You must be aware, Rob, that Lance Edwards has been trailing you with a dogged persistence. Doesn't it bother you?"

"Not really," said Rob mildly. "There's something about the man, something oddly familiar. I feel some sort of connection there—as if, given half a chance, the two of us could be friends."

"You can't be serious."

"But I am. I sense something in him. Something's hounding him, Michelle, just like my past is oppressing me. I feel—I don't know what to call it—a strange sort of alliance with the man—as if we're both actually after the same thing."

"That makes no sense, Rob. He's a cold, calculating reporter out for a story. He doesn't care who he hurts in the process."

Eventually during our San Diego drives, Rob and I began to communicate on an even deeper level, to talk about our feelings, our hopes, even our fears. I talked about my dream of someday writing the Great American Novel while Rob wondered aloud, with a sad kind of irony, what his own talents might have been.

"Music, for one," I told him. "You play beautifully—and you love it. You spend hours at the piano when you think no one is listening."

"Music is the nearest I come to freedom," he mumbled cryptically. "I feel the closest to being myself—whoever I am."

Sharing still didn't come easily for Rob. I understood. After all, what could a man talk about who had no memory, no identity? One gray, overcast day in mid-February, as we drove south through San

Clemente, Rob blurted out, "I feel like I'm part of some hideous masquerade, Michelle."

Keeping my gaze on the road ahead, I asked cautiously, "What do you mean?"

Frustration colored his tone. "I go along playing the role, pretending to be Rob Thornton, trying to anticipate what he—whoever he was—might do or say. But the fact is I'm not him—not here inside where I think and feel."

I grasped for the right words. "But, Rob, like your mom and David say, as soon as your memory returns—"

"What you don't understand, Michelle, is that David and Eva live with an external set of facts. People—strangers I don't even know—told them I'm Rob Thornton, but in my head I live with another set of facts, and those facts tell me I'm Cory Rugby. You tell me, Michelle, who's right?"

"You can't argue with the evidence, Rob," I ventured.

"Can't I? Even Washington can make a mistake. I've thought about it over and over, Michelle. It's been over twelve years. My hands were burned, my fingerprints practically obliterated. Who's to say there wasn't a mix-up somewhere along the line? It's my life, and everyone is forcing me into a mold that doesn't fit. I don't know how much longer I can play this game, this blasted charade. I just wish I'd never heard the name Rob Thornton!"

"But your memory—"

"Stop it, Michelle. Don't be like the others. That's all I hear anymore—when you remember, when you remember! God help me, Michelle, all I remember is Cory Rugby. All I want to do is get on with living, being the man I choose to be, not locked into someone else's identity or tied to a past I can't even recall. I've been a prisoner long enough."

"I just wish there was some way I could help you, Rob—to let you truly be yourself. But all I know is writing."

He stared out the car window. Down the cliff to our right, the Pacific Ocean thrashed tempestuously against the shoreline. "I feel like that ocean," he declared, "void and endless...anonymous."

"I look at the ocean and want to write," I said wistfully. Rob's silence made me feel apologetic, as if I had no right to share my dreams. I could feel his eyes on me. Were they angry? Probing? Challenging me? "What are you thinking?" I asked.

"About your writing. I was wondering...why don't you write about me—tell my story—"

"Are you serious?"

"I don't know." He shook his head in genuine bafflement. "It's crazy, Michelle. At times I begin to feel that the man I know myself to be and this other man, Rob Thornton, will merge as one and the confusion will be over." His words were coming now in short, urgent gasps. "At other times, everything feels so distant, disconnected. Do you know what it's like not to feel connected to another human soul...not even your own?"

I glanced at him with concern, then back at the road. "How do you think my writing your story could help?"

Rob's voice grew fervent. "You can create my identity, Michelle. When the flashes of insight come—the slivers of memory, the fleeting glimmers of recollection—you can write them down—"

Startlingly, I was beginning to catch Rob's sudden,

ardent compulsion. "Yes, I could piece them together—"

"—Like a jigsaw puzzle!"

"You know, it just might work, Rob. The answer's there. Surely the two of us can find it."

"And you won't run out on me, Michelle? You won't recoil at the secrets buried inside me?"

"Do you really think I would?"

He was pensive as I drove into the parking lot at the Naval Hospital. Turning off the ignition, I pulled my writer's notebook from my purse, then twisted in the seat to face Rob. "Every little thing you remember, Rob, we'll write it down. It won't matter how insignificant it may seem to you, we'll get it all down."

"It's all so fragmented, Michelle. Quick little flashes. Thoughts that might have been. Something I see or hear that makes me think I've been there before—or heard it somewhere else. Then it's as if the wind catches it away and it's gone."

I tapped my notebook meaningfully. "We'll snatch it back from the wind," I promised. "We'll write down every fragment, Rob." I kept my voice controlled, feigned composure, desperately trying to hide the excitement that was building inside me. I was already remembering clues that had dropped along the way since Rob came home. I'd get those on paper later. The thought of helping Rob back to mental health pulsated through me. In a way I would be paying Eva back for all her generosity. And, oh, to do something for David—to show him how much I loved him by helping his friend!

Rob and I left the car and walked through the sentry gate. The guard waved us on toward the wide cement steps that led up a sloping, grassy hillside toward the Administration Building. Rob lingered at the middle level by an old-fashioned cannon, a Naval Howitzer. "Looks like some of my buddies once used this," Rob told me.

"Your buddies?"

He nodded at the plaque at the base of the cannon. "Yeah. U.S. Marines."

One of the jigsaw pieces, I thought. *Rugby—U.S. Marines. Thornton—U.S. Navy.*

Rob's gaze wandered beyond the cannon, past the green rail fence. He studied the hazy skyline, then said, "San Diego and the Coronado Bridge were some of the last sites I saw when we pulled out for Nam. Boy, we were young and scared and gutsy and so sure we'd finish the job and be right back, pick up our lives. . . ."

"You sailed from here?" I asked, knowing that Rob had.

"Yeah," he answered. "It's crazy. Mom came to California to spend a few days with me before I sailed. I promised her I'd be back someday . . ." A quizzical expression flashed across his face. "I really did. For an instant it was so clear—a woman standing there in a blue suit with flowers in her hand."

"Was it Eva?"

"I don't know. I could hear her crying, but her face was bent, hidden in the flowers."

I felt a sudden, throat-catching tenderness. Touching his arm gently, I said, "It's time for your appointment with the psychiatrist. I'll wait for you in the chapel." I nodded toward the small adobe-white building nearby.

He squared his shoulders. "I'm not going, Michelle."

"You have to, Rob. You're—you're still Navy. Still under orders."

"I'm not going." He was in one of his mood swings, restless, resentful. "I'm sick of those counseling sessions, Michelle," he complained. "They're useless. Over and over the same questions."

"Your doctor is just trying to help you."

"I'm supposed to snap to with twelve years?" He clicked his fingers. "Tell me, Lieutenant," he mocked, "what happened after the crash? . . . . Where were you imprisoned? . . . . How did you escape? . . . . Who was with you? . . . ."

Rob's eyes were blazing now. "Tell me, Michelle, can you spill out everything about your last twelve years? Nonstop, no mistakes?"

I smiled inwardly. "That would take me back to my pigtail days. You wouldn't want to know about those."

Rob touched my hair and pushed it back from my face. "I want to know everything about you, Michelle."

An alarm button sounded a warning signal inside me. "Go to your appointment," I urged. "If we're going to write this book, I need your doctor's permission. I want you to ask him—"

"Definitely not."

"Rob, I don't want to do anything that might harm you."

"You won't harm me, Liana."

I looked up sharply. "I'm Michelle, remember?"

"I know. I don't know why I call you that. I guess you remind me of her."

"Will you tell me about her someday?"

"Yes, I want to . . . someday."

"And I'll be ready to listen," I answered. I gave

him a gentle shove. "But for now, your doctor is waiting."

Still he hesitated. "Michelle, will you help me find my real family?"

The question had come out of the blue, catching me unaware. I felt as if I were deceiving, betraying David and Eva when I answered, "I'll do my best."

Rob took my hand and pressed it against his lips, then said feverishly, "Do you know, Michelle, if it weren't for you—these days together—I'd have nothing to live for. I can't measure up to Eva and David's expectations. I know I'm disappointing them. I'm trying so hard to remember. I want my memory back so I can prove to everyone I'm Cory Rugby, not Rob Thornton. Yet, sometimes, I don't want to remember. It's too painful, too frightening."

I drew back, feeling suddenly overwhelmed by the intensity of Rob's emotions. "Please, don't give up, Rob. You have everything to live for." We stood gazing at each other, mute and motionless for a long moment before I turned away. "I'm going to the chapel," I said.

"To pray?"

"To wait for you. It's quiet. I like being alone. And, well, yes, actually I'll pray for you while you're having your session."

He started to walk away, then turned back and smiled—a captivating smile, those probing eyes studying me intently. "For you," he said candidly, "I could even pray. Anything to be with you."

I pivoted and walked briskly to the chapel—my favorite haven while I waited for Rob. It was a paneled, austere room with a well-worn gold rug, a small organ and podium, and three stained-glass windows. I slipped past the five rows of chairs to the table at the front with its ornate, carved metal cross. A large King James Bible lay open to John 14. My eyes settled on a phrase: "Let not your heart be troubled; neither let it be afraid."

I turned to the nearest chair and dropped to my knees, covering my mouth to muffle my cry. "Oh, God. I don't want to rush ahead of You. If You want me to write Rob's story... if it will help him... but don't let him mistake my care and concern for deeper affection. If we write this book, Lord, it will take time, more time away from David...."

I heard the chaplain's door open behind me and the floor squeaking as someone came toward me. "Can I help?" a voice asked. "I'm Chaplain Crawford."

I looked up at the slim, sandy-haired chaplain— an immaculate, fortyish man with a warm, riveting gaze and a thin layer of freckly skin stretched over his bony features. He helped me to my feet and sat down beside me.

"Is your loved one ill?" he asked in his clipped Eastern accent.

"Not my loved one," I stammered. "A friend. Lt. Rob Thornton."

His sagacious eyes brightened with recognition. "No wonder you look familiar. How is Lt. Thornton?"

"You don't know?"

He smiled with a trace of amusement. "I thought you might add to what I do know."

I was about to roll off a typical inane response— *He's fine, thank you. We're all just fine*—when rashly, impetuously, I began pouring out the truth. I told Chaplain Crawford about the book Rob wanted me to write, about my fears, about the tensions at home, the constant rifts and irritations—and, just minutes ago, the warning signal inside me. "I'm engaged and I'm not certain what I should do... whether I should spend so much time with Rob—"

The chaplain glanced at my ring finger.

"I'll be getting a ring," I said hastily, "once everything's settled with Lt. Thornton...."

"But not from Lt. Thornton?"

"Oh, no. From David Ballard. Perhaps you remember him from the family conference last December when Rob came home."

"Yes. Very well." A knowing smile passed across the chaplain's face. "And you think if you write Lt. Thornton's story, you'll be free to go on with your wedding?" He didn't wait for my reply. "But you're afraid of more involvement with the Lieutenant than your fiance would approve of, aren't you?"

I nodded, surprised that he could take my tumbling, incoherent phrases, my inner thoughts, and couch them in words. "I really think God wants me to write Rob's story, but lately David—that's my fiance—thinks I'm paying more attention to Rob than I should. It's almost as though he's—"

"Jealous?" the chaplain surmised.

"Oh, Chaplain Crawford, it's not like David to be jealous. He's such a godly man."

"And you don't think that Abraham and Moses and Paul were ever jealous?" He stood up and offered me his hand. "I can't make your decision for you, Miss Merrill. But I will pray. Now if you'll excuse me, I have another appointment. But if I can be of any further help..."

I was beginning to wish I had the chaplain's help when Rob arrived minutes later. Rob was more agitated than he had ever been after a counseling session. He paced back and forth in the small chapel, rearranging the rows of chairs, pulling tracts from the rack. Then he whirled around and shouted, "Names, names! That's what the 'shrink' wants. The names of those who were in prison with me. But, Michelle, I spent so much time alone, I don't even know the names."

"Alone?" I asked softly. "Were you in isolation?"

I had the feeling he was remembering, groping for one jagged piece of the puzzle. Then, as quickly, he was mentally running, withdrawing, his face ashen, the memories too distressing to put into words, the elusive details evaporating like mist.

"Rob," I coaxed gently, "can you tell me about the other Americans with you? There were others with you over the years, weren't there?"

"Different ones," he said tonelessly. "But there were two men—we were together a lot." He stopped by the middle stained-glass window portraying the cross and the crown. I went to him and read the words engraved on the window: " 'Lord, hear us as we lift our prayers for those in peril in the air.' Rob, that's a prayer for Navy pilots and navigators. . . ."

"And those still in prison?" he asked bitterly.

"Yourself?" I asked. "Or those two friends in POW camps with you?"

He shrugged. "All of us, I guess." He wheeled and gazed down at me. There was a palpating twitch by his mouth that I hadn't noticed before. Was he trying to say something? "Rob, do you remember your friends' names?" I prodded.

He shook his head mechanically. "No names. Everything's time-juggled, out of kilter. There was a Marine and a civilian. The civilian was a . . . missionary. That's it, a missionary. A religious guy."

Rob's gaze revealed a tantalizing sense of recognition. "Dick something. Dick Evans. That's it, Michelle. The civilian's name was Dick Evans." His face clouded again. "I don't remember the other guy's name. Just when I think I've got a handle on it, he kind of fades away. A tall, gaunt guy—dark hair and callused bare feet. I keep seeing him, hunched a little, in that peasant outfit they made us wear." He drew in a breath. "And, Michelle, I think he came from a military family. He was always talking about his dad, the Colonel."

"Rob, do you remember anything else about him? Was he injured?"

"I don't know, Michelle. He made a crude crutch, fashioned it out of something—a tree limb? I don't know who it was for."

I waited, unmoving. The chapel was as quiet as I had ever heard it. I was almost afraid to breathe, to break Rob's reverie.

"You know, we used to mark off the days and months on that old crutch." Rob's eyes softened. "The missionary marked off the days with prayer."

I remained silent, listening. I felt an inexorable mixture of anguish and anticipation as I watched reality and illusion collide in Rob's expression.

"Michelle, I was scared. I wanted to escape the prison camp. I have this nightmare—I think I planned to turn against my friends. In my mind I heard someone saying, 'Man, don't sell your soul for a bowl of rice and a cigarette.' "

I watched him, puzzled. Eva and David had both said Rob never smoked. "What happened to your friends?" I asked.

"I don't know, Michelle. They must be dead." Again he withdrew. It was obvious that the answer

was there, inside Rob, but buried too deep for perhaps anyone to reach. Or did he know more than
he was saying? Was he afraid to tell the truth? Had
he actually considered selling out? Hadn't every
POW been pushed beyond his limit? "Let's go home,
Rob," I suggested. "It's a long drive."

It was nippy and cold outside the chapel. An
afternoon storm was brewing. In the distance I could
see a slanting, translucent rain suffusing the sky
with a pallid glow. Just as we reached my Honda,
Rob stopped abruptly. "My psychiatrist reminds me
of the Vulture."

"The Vulture?"

"He was a madman—the short, runty interrogator
in one of the POW camps." Rob's words erupted in
a torrent. "The Vulture had dark beady eyes in a
leathery, beaklike face. I can see him now—his
scrawny neck thrust forward in a perpetual gesture
of searing scrutiny. He stood over us, unkempt in
his rumpled khaki uniform, his sleeves rolled up to
his bony elbows, screeching at us in a strident, high-
pitched shrill. Sometimes when the doctor's talking,
his face blurs and turns cruel, birdlike, threatening.
I imagine he's going to strike, beat me."

"Then you're saying you're afraid of your doctor?"

"Not exactly. But I am afraid of what he wants
me to tell him. He says I remember more than I'm
letting on."

"Is that true, Rob?"

His muscles tensed; his face twisted in a garish
mask of agony. He looked ready for combat. "It was
true—today, Michelle. I know certain things, but I
don't even know how I know them. I know I am
Cory Rugby, and—" His voice grew thin and brittle.
"God forgive me, I killed someone."

A stunned silence hung heavy between us. "But you were in a war," I stammered at last. "It was expected—"

"It wasn't the enemy, Michelle. It was someone I knew. I don't know who or how or when or why, but I'm carrying the terrible guilt of it, like a rock in my gut, so I know it's true."

Rob was alert and rational and I knew it. Something in his acid glare—in the way his dusky lips trembled—frightened me. He waved his cane aimlessly at the wind. "What can I do, Michelle?" he uttered in desolation.

I groped at straws. "Perhaps you should tell your psychiatrist."

"And what do you think the Navy would do, Michelle? Pat me on the shoulder and tell me everything will be okay? I can't tell them anything! I don't want to go back to prison." His words caught in his throat. "Or be locked up in some psychiatric ward!"

"We'll work it out, Rob," I said with far more confidence than I felt. Even as I slipped into the driver's seat, I knew the rainstorm would hit before we reached Irvine. But what was worse, for a terrible, fleeting instant, I wondered if I was safe driving home alone with Rob Thornton.

CHAPTER
THIRTEEN

I killed someone. I carry the guilt of it in my gut always.

Rob's words plagued my mind constantly. Should I tell someone? David? Eva? Rob's psychiatrist? Commander Thomas?

I thought suddenly of Lance Edwards. Was this the dread, unspeakable secret he was pursuing so relentlessly? What did Edwards already know about Rob to make him such a fierce adversary? What did he discover in Thailand at Rob's release to stir such antagonism, such enmity against Rob?

I wondered how much information Lance had insidiously gleaned from Pam during their increasingly frequent dates. Whenever I tried to ask Pam about her evenings out with Lance, she brushed me off with a tittering chuckle. "He's just a friend, Michelle—he's been everywhere, he's so worldly, sophisticated—"

"Worldly anyway," I muttered.

"Best of all, he loves to spend money..."

That was as far as our conversations went. I realized I'd never find out from Pam what Lance was up to. Perhaps she honestly didn't know. I couldn't imagine that she would deliberately side with him against Rob. Still, I had Lance pegged as a wily, crafty fellow not above schemes and tricks to procure his deadly exposés.

Lately even David seemed to be listening with a detached curiosity to Lance's innuendoes and insinuations, wondering—he told me privately—whether Lance might have substantial evidence or leads regarding Rob's long years in Indochina.

Several times when David and I were alone, I almost blurted out what Rob had told me in confidence: *I killed someone—not an enemy—someone I knew*. But always, just as I was about to speak, the words receded in my throat and I remained silent. I couldn't risk betraying Rob. He alone would have to be the one to tell David. And Eva. Everyone.

No matter how many times I told myself that Rob had a potential for violence, I couldn't get away from the gentle, deep warmth etched in his face as well. The protective mask that he had worn since coming home was slowly giving way to a trust and confidence when we were together. He was an extraordinarily caring person under it all, and though his smoldering fury frightened me, it also intrigued me. I felt cornered, inescapably committed to completing Rob's story and helping him find his roots.

I knew allowing the possibility that Rob was indeed someone else was a breech of David and Eva's faith in me. Perhaps even worse, I was inferring that the Navy had made a monumental error. But hadn't David assured me that was impossible?

In spite of my deepening inner conflict, my

manuscript file on Rob was growing rapidly. It was amazing what facts we had already accumulated—a far larger piece of the puzzle than we had anticipated. We knew now that Rob had been held prisoner in several POW camps in North Vietnam . . . had survived varying degrees of mistreatment and unbearable loneliness . . . that years after America's withdrawal, Rob had been interned with South Vietnamese political prisoners in a reeducation camp and had eventually escaped into Laos where he had been living for nearly four years.

But even with all this information, we still didn't have the slightest lead on Cory Rugby, and the Navy was adamant in their refusal to provide even the most innocuous details. We knew simply that Rugby was an MIA, a Marine Captain, a helicopter pilot. Where he lived, where he had come from, where he was shot down, and whether he had a family—a wife or children—was kept from us.

I had written letters to several POW-MIA groups, the state senator, and the congressman of our district. I'd haunted the local librarian, who insisted, "I can't help unless you know the young man's hometown. Then you could correspond with the librarian there. She might be able to help you uncover something from the newspaper stacks. Or the court records."

With or without information on Cory Rugby, I proceeded to write Rob's story. Lately I'd been spending long hours at Eva's desk in the living room—the only private corner I could find in the early morning when the others were sleeping. Eva's quaint George Washington-style desk, a five-sided polygon made of polished cherrywood, was tucked in the three-cornered window nook. The desk fired my writer's imagination and took me back to the early days of our country when Washington and Jefferson sat behind similar desks scratching on parchment with their feather pens.

Today, after our exhausting, traffic-clogged trip to San Diego, Eva's desk and the cozy living room were an especially welcome haven. I was so weary of those daily drives. If only I could sit here in comfort every day and write!

Suddenly Rob, looking far more energetic than I felt, burst into the room in his sweat suit, his face flushed with perspiration. "A hundred pushups," he announced.

I set down my pen, noting how nicely Rob was filling out. He was no longer bony and gaunt. "We were supposed to be working on your story," I scolded mildly.

"I'm working on my physique," he teased. "The physical therapist told me today he'll discharge me as soon as I begin an exercise program at home."

"Wonderful. That'll mean fewer drives to the hospital."

"Right," he replied, sobering momentarily. Then he brightened. "I'll still need a good chauffeur, Michelle. I'm taking Dave up on that athletic club membership. The therapist thinks swimming would be good for me."

"You must be an excellent swimmer—with all those trophies in your room."

He gave me a crooked grin. "You mean Thornton's trophies?"

"Does it matter—as long as you can swim?"

"That's one of those normal, automatic things you never forget—like driving a car. I know I can drive even though I can't remember ever having driven."

He smiled cannily. "Of course you won't let me prove it to you."

"You know Eva has promised you a car as soon as you're cleared medically," I reminded him.

"I told you, I'll buy my own car. I'm saving my Navy pay."

I handed Rob the papers I'd been working on. "These are the notes we have so far on your years in Laos."

He pulled a chair over beside me. "Those were my only half decent years over there," he reflected.

"You mean, because of. . .Liana?"

He nodded, then sat for several minutes in reflective silence before going on. "My clearest memory is of Liana. The first time I saw her, she was leaning over me sponging my face—the gentlest of hands touching me. I'd been sick, feverish with my first bout of cerebral malaria. There she was, her shiny black hair hanging down, partly hiding one eye. I reached up, weak and awkward, and pushed those strands of silk away from her face."

For a moment I thought Rob might cry. I reached over and squeezed his hand encouragingly.

"Michelle, she was such a beautiful young girl with doe-brown eyes, perfect skin, a graceful form. That day I traced her features, her soft lips and slender neck—knowing but not knowing how I knew—that I had not touched a woman for years. I could not remember the day before or the weeks or years. Only that moment."

"*Corree Rugbee*," she said in her lilting, singsong voice," Rob continued. "They were her first words to me. I don't think she ever called me just Cory, always *Corree Rugbee*."

I was afraid to break in with questions. For the

first time since I had known Rob, the tenderness that he so carefully guarded registered in his expression and voice. Did he know he loved Liana? I was sure he did. "What was she like?" I asked.

His icy blue eyes melted with memory. "She had a sweet shyness about her, like so many of the girls in the village. But that first day Liana never turned away, never lowered her gaze. I felt as if she had been studying me for hours. She stayed by my mat for days, feeding me a thin rice broth until I gained my strength. When I finally tried to walk, she served as my crutch until her people fashioned me a cane out of bamboo. Liana was a dainty, fawnlike girl with a spirited gait. She wore colorful embroidered skirts with intricate Chinese designs—mouse tracks, fish scales, and caterpillar prints.

"When I was well again," continued Rob, "I learned that I had been found near some caves and carried to the village hilltop by the Hmong people. They sheltered me, protected me. Isolated as we were, we were surprisingly safe from the Communist rule in the land. In time, because of Liana, I was accepted by her people. I learned their language, settled into their culture, and used my skills to devise a water wheel and a better drainage system for the village. In turn, in spite of my bum leg and physical frailty from my years in the prison camps, I learned to work side by side with the Hmong men, harvesting fields of corn and rice and raising a thatched hut in a single day."

"Weren't you eager to get home to the States?" I asked.

Rob sat doodling a row of numbers over and over on the manuscript folder. "For a long time I remembered nothing from the past," he said. "Deep inside,

I yearned for something familiar, something I couldn't even articulate. I knew I was an American. I knew my name was Cory Rugby. I knew I had fought in Vietnam. But beyond that, there was nothing. And even now, it comes back only in bits and pieces."

Rob and I talked for another hour, until Eva arrived home, ill with a migraine. I fixed her a cup of tea and shooed her off to bed.

While I was attending to Eva, Rob remained at the desk, reading my notes. "Do you want to work some more after dinner, Michelle?" he asked, sounding hopeful.

"I can't, Rob. David's coming over later for pizza."

He grimaced slightly. "Then I'm on my own for dinner?"

"You're welcome to join us, or if you're hungry, I'll fix you a sandwich now."

"I'll take my sandwich here at the desk while I read," he said tartly.

I brought Rob a ham sandwich and a glass of milk, assuring him, "We'll work on your story some more tomorrow."

David arrived shortly after nine, still in his gray pin-striped suit, smelling faintly of aftershave and spearmint gum. "Sorry I'm late, hon," he said breezily. "The work at the office was piled a mile high."

I kissed him on the lips. "It's okay. This is our *late* date, remember?"

He glanced into the living room where Rob was sitting at Eva's desk. "How's it going, Rob?"

Rob looked over, then tapped his sheaf of papers, straightening them. "Going all right, Dave. You?"

"Fine—wiped out. Typical day, you know?"

"Sure. Me, too."

David walked over and tossed his coat on the sofa, then turned to Rob. "Whatcha reading?"

Rob quickly slipped the papers into a manila envelope. "Notes—nothing really."

David glanced at me. "The book?"

I shrugged uncomfortably. "Yes. Rob was recalling his years in Laos. I tried to get everything down."

"You're doing a good job, Michelle," Rob assured me. "You word everything so much better than I— beautifully!"

"So!" said David with a hefty sigh. "When do I get to read this masterpiece?"

I felt my face coloring. "It's not a finished manuscript, David. It's only a very rough draft. It's far from complete."

Rob strode across the room, the envelope tucked securely under his arm. "I'll leave you two now to your visit. Good night, Dave."

"Hey, old man, no need to go on my account."

"You're welcome to join us, Rob," I said halfheartedly. "Like I told you, we're just going to fix pizza and watch the late show."

Rob gave me a lingering glance. "Thanks, Michelle. I'd love to, but . . ." He eyed David. "I had her all day, man. It's your turn, right?"

"You bet, buddy." David wasn't smiling.

Passing by, Rob touched my shoulder lightly. "I'll finish reading these in my room. See you in the morning, Michelle."

David paced the room, looking restless, until we heard Rob's door click shut. Then, loosening his tie, he asked, "Where's Eva?"

"She went to bed a couple of hours ago. Had one

of those migraine headaches she's been getting lately."

David nodded. "I saw it coming on at work. I told her to go home early, but she wouldn't do it."

"Well, I fixed her some tea and sent her to bed. I think she just needed someone to take charge and insist she rest."

"Good. That's the only way you can handle Eva." He looked around. "So where's Pam?"

I scowled. "Out with Lance Edwards—again."

David's brows arched. "Really? Looking serious, huh?"

"Oh, Shakespeare—I hope not!" I hesitated. "David, would it bother you—Pam and Lance?"

He shrugged. "I never thought much about it."

"But you like Pam—"

"Sure, she's your kid sister—"

"You and Pam have so much in common...and you seem to hit it off so well."

David gripped my shoulders. "Listen, my sweet darling, I've been kind to Pam, thinking it was what you wanted—"

"I do, of course I do, but when the two of you talk about work, about things I know nothing about anymore, I feel...left out."

Merriment played in David's eyes. "Pam can never match you, Michelle. She lacks your artistic sensitivity, your depth, your compassion. Sure, she can talk math and computers, but she's surface level—not the quality I see in you."

I bit my lower lip to keep it from quivering. "A-Are you sure?"

"Positive." He was silent a moment, obviously mulling over something noteworthy. "You know, sweetheart," he said at last, "I've got the money to give you just about whatever you want, but if I lost everything tomorrow—if I were poverty-stricken—I believe you'd still love me without question."

"Just one question," I smiled seductively. "If you do go broke, can I lend you a few dollars for our marriage license?"

He drew me into his arms. "I think that could be arranged. Now please, Michelle, don't let Pam's innocent little flirtations bother you."

Slowly I removed his tie and draped it over the sofa. "Let's not talk about Pam anymore tonight. I'm in a wonderful mood and don't want to spoil it."

David kissed my eyelids, the tip of my nose. "Tell me, what brought on this terrific mood of yours?"

"You—and knowing we have this whole evening together."

His mouth moved over my face and hair. "My mood...is improving...by the minute," he murmured, "now that I have you...all to myself."

"First, the pizza, David," I teased, wriggling free.

"Pizza?"

"I promised you homemade pizza—the works!—and what I promise, I deliver."

"I'll keep that in mind," he winked, following me to the kitchen.

I showed him my fresh, ready-to-bake creation. "Mushrooms, pepperoni, olives, sausage, and two kinds of cheese," I announced proudly. "This pizza's got it all."

David plucked up an anchovy and examined it. "And, I dare say, a few items that haven't even been invented yet."

"Everything but onions," I said meaningfully.

"You did think of everything," he mused, stifling a grin.

I slid the pizza into the hot oven and set the timer. Then, arm in arm, we strolled back to the living room. "You mentioned the late show?" he asked.

"Actually, the early-late show. Alfred Hitchcock's *Suspicion.*"

"That's an old one."

"Nineteen-forty-one. Cary Grant, Joan Fontaine— my favorites."

"That charming little tale about the bride who suspects her husband of trying to kill her?"

I kissed his cheek. "Right. You're marvelous at trivia, darling."

He fluffed the sofa pillows and sat down, pulling me down beside him. "A pleasant little romantic comedy would have been more in keeping with our mood . . ."

I feigned a pout. "But you know how I love intrigue."

"You thrive on intrigue, Michelle, and I thrive on you. So I guess I'll just have to get used to a wife who prefers dashing off descriptions in her writer's notebook to dashing off fancy dishes in the kitchen."

I pretended indignation. "How soon you forget my remarkable pizza!"

David sat forward, sniffing the air. "I think maybe *you* forgot the pizza."

I jumped up and rushed to the kitchen. "If it's burned, we call out for Chinese."

David was right behind me. "Are you kidding? I've got a stake in this little bit of Italy. I won't rest until I figure out what those curly pink things were swimming in the mozzarella."

"Shrimp, if you must know." I pulled on my thick oven mitts and carefully lifted the bubbly, golden brown pizza over to the counter. "Perfect," I announced smugly.

"Yeah, well," grumped David mockingly, "my specialty is steaks."

"I remember. You broiled steaks for us in Morro Bay."

"They weren't so bad. Maybe not exactly rare—"

"Rare? Really, David! I had my choice of cuts—singed, charred, or ashes!"

"So I'm not the world's greatest chef?" He wrapped me in his arms and said huskily, "I can't even promise to be the world's greatest lover, Michelle. But I'll love you with all my heart all the days of my life."

"Please remember those words of endearment," I whispered. "I want to hear them all over again right after our pizza."

Following our little impromptu dinner, David and I spent a blissful evening pretending to watch TV but gradually, inevitably growing more absorbed in each other than in Grant and Fontaine. After the movie, David turned on the stereo and stoked the dying embers in the fireplace. We relaxed in the darkened room, our heads together, dreamily distracted by the crackling, dancing flames.

"This is how it should always be," he said softly.

"I've never felt so happy, David."

"Me neither, Michelle. I'm counting the days until you're completely mine."

"Really? Just how many—"

A shrill, ear-piercing scream split the air.

I sat forward, my heart pounding madly.

"What on earth was that?" cried David.

"Rob." I stood up, tense, a sudden metallic taste in my mouth.

David caught my hand. "Where are you going,

Michelle?"

"He's having one of his nightmares. I've got to—"

"You can't run to him every time he cries out in his sleep."

I pulled my hand free. "Maybe I can help—"

"Rob's got to work it out himself!"

"But he's immobilized by those nightmarish flashbacks. They terrify him, David."

"Then let Eva go to him. It's a mother's job."

"He won't want Eva."

"I don't care what he wants. You were with him all day. In fact, lately you spend more time with him than you do with me."

I was already taking long strides toward the hallway. "Please understand—he needs me, David."

I heard David utter caustically, "What about me, Michelle? I need you too!"

CHAPTER FOURTEEN

David was ready to leave when I returned from Rob's room.

"You don't have to go yet," I told him. "Rob's asleep. He just had another of his nightmares."

David looked tired, distracted. "It's late, Michelle. We'd better call it a night."

I nodded, disappointed, realizing that the lovely, fragile spell of the evening had been broken. "See you tomorrow?"

"Maybe."

I handed him his tie. "Eva mentioned having a brunch on Saturday—her special strawberry waffles. You'll come, won't you?"

"Sure, why not?" David tossed the tie around his neck, then kissed my cheek lightly. "Night, hon."

After David left I fled to my room and gave vent to a rush of unreasoning tears. I wasn't sure what had happened between David and me just now. Things had been so good, then incomprehensively they somersaulted, leaving an immovable barrier between us.

Rob again, I reflected darkly. Lately it was always Rob. He had become a constant, unwitting irritant, provoking David, chafing and ruffling our once tranquil relationship.

My anger flared momentarily against Rob, then settled sulkingly on David. Why couldn't David be more understanding? After all, Rob was his friend. It hadn't been my idea to get involved in Rob's recovery. But now that I was involved, I had to see it through. Did David really want me to desert Rob during this critical time when Rob's condition was so tenuous, his self-image so vulnerable?

At last, my tears spent, I undressed, slipped into my silk nightgown, and climbed into bed. For a change, I was glad Pam wasn't home yet. I needed these rare moments of privacy. More important, I didn't want Pam writing home to Mom and Dad about the growing tensions between David and me.

I drifted into an uneasy sleep, down, down into murky, exhausted slumber. Then...something stirred...drawing me back from distant, diaphanous dreams.

Someone.

I opened my eyes. Darkness. Silence. No—a rustle. Movement—barely perceptible. A form hovered over me—a shadowy silhouette against the less opaque filigrees of night.

My breath caught. My muscles tensed with alarm, an electric current shooting through my nerve endings.

"Liana?" Rob's voice.

I tried to speak. My thoughts were still sleep-clogged, my mouth sawdust-dry, my reflexes a beat too slow.

Rob bent down and gathered me into his arms.

"Rob, no!" I protested, twisting out of his embrace.

He drew me against him, relentless, his voice soft and urgent. "You left me, Liana. Why did you go? Why did you run away? I thought you loved me. You do love me, don't you, Liana?"

I pressed my palms against Rob's chest and pushed. The room was flooded suddenly with light. I blinked against the blinding brightness. Pam stood in the doorway, her hand still on the light switch, staring back at Rob and me in stunned silence.

Rob jumped up awkwardly, his face contorted with shame and bafflement as he gazed with a pitiful desperation from Pam to me. "Michelle, I didn't know—I just—I'm sorry—!"

I sat up, pulling the covers around my shoulders, and looked helplessly at Pam.

"Oh, Michelle!" she gasped.

Rob brushed past her and darted out of the room.

Pam hurried over and sat beside me on the bed. "Are you—all right, Michelle?"

"Yes, of course. I—I just—"

"Did he hurt you?"

"No!—Rob?—He wouldn't—he just—he must have been dreaming—sleepwalking—"

Pam shook her head dubiously. In a hushed, horrified voice, she asked, "What would have happened if I hadn't come home just now, Michelle?"

"Nothing, Pam," I scoffed, shivering a little. "Nothing would have happened. Rob wouldn't harm me."

Pam stood up and shut the door firmly. "You don't

know that, Michelle. You're so trusting. You believe what you want to believe. You'd better watch your step around Rob. He's still not well. And he's becoming obsessed with you. Be careful, you hear?"

I wanted to assure Pam that I wasn't Rob's obsession; it was a young woman named Liana on the other side of the globe. But it was too late tonight to delve into the matter, so instead, I quelled my lingering tremors and asked, "How was your evening with Lance?"

"Obviously not as cozy as yours with Rob," she said with concerned irony.

On Saturday I tried to put my nagging frustrations about David and Rob out of my mind as Pam and I helped Eva prepare brunch. Eva served her luscious strawberry waffles while Pam and I rounded out the meal with our special sausage and mushroom omelet. To our delight, David and Rob ate heartily. Even more satisfying was the fact that they seemed to be enjoying each other's company for the first time in weeks. I was glad now that I had refrained from telling David about Rob's disturbing visit to my room. What purpose would it have served, especially since Rob and I hadn't even discussed it? In fact, I wasn't even sure Rob recalled the incident.

The conversation around the table remained light and pleasant for most of our brunch. Then, gradually, it turned to more sober matters as David and Eva reminisced about the past. Rob looked uneasy. He sat in self-absorbed silence, doodling on his paper napkin—the same numbers he had written on the manuscript folder last week. But when David brought up the subject of Vietnam, Rob immediately snapped to attention, his gaze riveting on David.

"I keep hoping you'll remember our last flight

together, Rob. Any of the flights, for that matter."

"What's so special about the last one? Crashing?" That strange expression crossed Rob's face—distraught, quizzical.

"Every flight was special, Rob. We had a good buddy relationship. You did a lot of bragging—but I didn't mind. It's what kept you going. Kept you laughing. Kept you dreaming."

"Who dreams during a war?" Rob challenged.

"We all did," said David, indulging in a rare moment of retrospection. "About survival mostly, about getting home."

Rob turned his head slightly, a mechanical, slow-motion rerun—his profile intense, handsome, and finely carved from his arched brow to his neatly trimmed beard. I wondered if his thoughts were moving at the same mechanical pace. "Buddies, huh?" he asked, mulling over the idea as if it were somehow appealing, as though having had a friend high over Hanoi was important to him even now. "What kind of things did I trust you with, Dave?"

"You shared everything—your home life, Purdue, the girls, your trophies." An unexpected tenderness softened David's tone. "But what impressed me most was the way you talked so freely and proudly about your mother. You had stacks of letters from her, wrapped together. You'd read every one of them to me. They stirred an emptiness in the pit of my gut. My folks were dead. Cheryl, my girl, had dumped me, so you offered me a place in your family. Big brother, you called me. Mom can handle a second son, you said. She's loaded with love."

"You handled that position fairly well in my absence," Rob said coolly. There was a fractional grimace, a flash of resentment in his eyes, like a camera shutter snapping, catching each emotion as it changed Rob's expression. "Mom couldn't have got along without you."

Eva bit her lower lip, checking a quiver that played there now.

Streaks of crimson marked David's neckline. "I looked Eva up because of a promise I made to you, Rob."

"On our last flight?" Rob asked sullenly, marking his napkin.

"Probably—whenever—"

"Did I ask you to take over, squeeze me out?"

David winced. "You told me if anything happened to you, to look up your mom, take care of her."

"And you didn't waste any time doing that."

Eva cut in, her voice taut. "Rob, David kept his promise to you. He came to me at a time when I was devastated. You were my whole life, Rob, and I thought you were gone."

"And I bet you wish I was still gone," he muttered.

Eva's eyes filled. She blinked, averting her gaze.

"Rob," I countered, "that's not fair."

"So what about it, Dave? What about our last flight together?"

David's brow furrowed slightly. "We were in our Phantom, Rob. I had an uneasy feeling about that flight. I'd be rotating out after another five missions. That meant you'd be staying on. I felt I had to take a shot in the dark. Push you for a decision. I said, 'Rob, I'm worried about you and your relationship with God. We may not make every mission. We've seen our friends go down, not come back. You really need to square things away, accept Christ.' "

"And what did I do?" Rob asked warily.

"You told me you were too young, had too much

living to do. You'd think about it when you got home."

Surprise registered in Eva's expression. "David, you never told me about that conversation with Rob."

"I didn't see what purpose it would serve, Eva."

Rob was studying David intently, as though way back somewhere he was remembering. "And what else did I say?"

"You told me that day that you wished you were back home, eating your mom's roasts and cookies and pies. You wanted to be back at Purdue University doing graduate work, back where you belonged. You said you could think more clearly about God when you got home. You're home now, man. What about it?"

"So now I'm thinking clearly?" His eyes were alert, piercing, as they might have been on that last flight with David, vigilant for enemy aircraft. Only now I sense that Rob considered us the enemy.

Stop, David, I cautioned silently. *Don't push now. The time's not right.*

But David went on amassing his verbal weaponry in much the same way he had stacked the snowballs at the cabin. He would throw his arguments one by one, with exquisite ease until he had Rob cornered.

As I refilled David's coffee cup, I touched him lightly on the shoulder, a warning gesture. He gave me a spurning glance and pushed on. "In Vietnam, you put God on the shelf, waiting for the perfect time. You're still doing that, Rob. Memory loss or no memory loss, you're still accountable."

Rob's ultramarine eyes seemed distant, troubled as he glanced across the table at David. "I don't have much to offer God, Dave. Frankly, I'm angry at Him—getting me into that hellish mess I lived in for years." He shrugged lamely. "I don't seem to be any better off right now. My surroundings, yes. God help me, they're beautiful. But I can't help feeling like everybody ran out on me."

"God didn't."

"Believe it or not, Dave, I'm just trying to sort out God and His claims. Over there in Nam—war and killing—they didn't help to make God real." Rob was tracing the numbers on his napkin again, turning the lines into bold, black distortions. "So what was your big message to me high over Hanoi?" he asked David.

"I'll tell you what I told you then, man. Thirty-seven minutes before that Vietnamese boy tossed the hand grenade that blew you out of my sight— but never my memory—thirty-seven minutes before that, I said, 'There won't be a better time or a bigger need than now, Rob. It's not where you are that counts but whether you know Christ.' "

When Rob remained stoically silent, David choked out the words, "I'm talking about redemption, man. Christ dying for you, redeeming you." The scar that cut across David's jawline pulsated. "I still feel the same way, Rob. I know we haven't been the best of friends lately. I know we find it difficult to talk, but there's nothing I want more for you today, man, than God's peace."

There was an eerie quietness in the room. I had the feeling that Eva was praying, praying again for her son. Pam—who lived life lightly, without commitments—seemed strangely moved. For once Rob was calm, listening, as though some inviolable hush had fallen upon him. I realized that he was seriously weighing David's words.

"I remember crashing, Dave," he murmured solemnly. "If you say these things are true, they must have been. I remember Dick Evans—the missionary in the prison camp—preaching and praying, whispering his spiritual concerns for me. But I can't remember anything you said. I can't even remember being with you."

David leaned back in his chair. "It's okay, Rob. I came on kind of heavy. I just wanted you to know . . ."

"Dave, I'm sorry. Really I'm sorry." Rob's voice was unusually mellow. "I don't think forgiveness can reach me." He sat forward, his head in his hands. Slowly his shoulders shook; sobs followed, his tears dropping unchecked on the tablecloth.

Eva went to him immediately. "It's all right, Rob. We won't press you." She touched him gently, lovingly. "We just want you to be at peace. There's only one way for that."

"Your God?" he mumbled.

Eva nodded. "You'll never know how much pain I felt over the years thinking that you had died without Christ."

Rob pushed away Eva's hand, scraped back his chair and stood, his face twisted in despair. "No more," he uttered. "I'm beyond redemption." The whipped cream and strawberries streamed a blood path across his plate. He glared angrily at us, then limped out of the room and down the hall. We heard his bedroom door shut soundly.

"Eva, I . . ." David looked helpless, boyishly abashed. "I blow it every time with Rob. I'm sorry."

"You meant well, David."

"It wasn't you, David," I assured him. "It's something far deeper. Something that happened in Southeast Asia."

"What? Do you know, Michelle?"

"I don't think even Rob knows completely."

Pam dipped a finger in the bowl of whipped cream and licked it. "I guess I ought to say something profound and medical," she offered lamely. "Like, 'He seems to be getting better.' But between his bouts of fury and his wandering uninvited into strange bedrooms—"

I kicked Pam under the table but it was too late.

"Doing what?" David and Eva asked together.

"It's nothing," I protested. "A little mix-up the other night."

"Did Rob come to your room—bother you?" David pressed. "Is that what Pam is saying?"

"Oh, my goodness, David," exclaimed Eva, "Rob would never—"

"He didn't hurt her, David," Pam spoke up. "I don't think he even knew what he was doing!"

David's eyes were mesmerizing. His gaze pinned me to the wall. "What happened, Michelle? Did Rob—surely he didn't—attack you?"

"No, David, of course not! He was dreaming—he thought I was someone else," I stammered. "He didn't hurt me."

The muscles around David's mouth contracted involuntarily. I could see rage erupting volcanically through the tendons and sinews of his face. "What did he do, Michelle?"

"Nothing! He—he—tried to kiss me. He thought I was Liana—!"

David threw his napkin into his plate. "It's gone

far enough," he stormed. "Rob belongs back in the hospital!"

Eva looked appalled. "No, David. He belongs here with us, with the people who love him!"

"He doesn't even know us, Eva," countered David. "He still thinks he's this Cory Rugby fellow."

"I don't care who he thinks he is. He's still my son. And he didn't hurt Michelle. She said so herself."

David's eyes narrowed with rancor. "He's not the Rob I knew. Can any of us be sure he's not dangerous, especially with those unpredictable flashbacks?"

"He would never hurt anyone, would he, Michelle?" Eva persisted, her voice rising shrilly.

"I—I can't imagine—," I said falteringly. *I killed someone, Michelle—not the enemy—someone I knew—*

Pam waved her hands helplessly. "I'm sorry I even mentioned—"

"I've been thinking," continued David, "and this confirms it—"

Eva rushed on, "We're all jumping to conclusions—"

"I think from now on," decided David stonily, "Eva or Pam should drive Rob to San Diego."

We all stopped and stared mutely at David.

At last I found my voice. "You don't want me driving Rob to the hospital anymore?"

David's gaze bore through me. "You've shouldered the responsibility long enough, Michelle. Eva's caught up on her work now. It's her place to be with her son. Or what about Pam? She's a nurse. Who would be better suited for Rob?"

My senses recoiled with a mixture of vexation and disbelief. "Rob trusts me, David. He needs me. I can't let him down."

"He's depending too much on you, Michelle."

"But I haven't finished writing his story—"

"You had no right to promise him that book. It's pure foolishness. What would his psychiatrist say—?"

Tears blurred my vision. "Please, David, let's not talk about this here—not now—"

David turned to Pam. "How about it, Pam? You wouldn't mind driving Rob to San Diego for his treatments, would you?"

Pam shrugged helplessly. "I—I guess not—"

"David, this is ridiculous," I declared hotly. "After all, Rob and I will still be living in the same house."

David sat back and drew in a sharp breath. "I suppose you can lock your door at night—"

"My bedroom door? Oh, David, really! There's no lock—"

"All right, I'll buy you one, install it myself—"

A deep masculine voice, raw and wounded, uttered: "That won't be necessary, Dave."

We all whirled around to see Rob in the doorway, his face blanched and desolate, his eyes glinting fire. "I'd never hurt Michelle," he thundered. "Never!"

A glacial chill settled over me, numbing my senses. The words wrenched from me: "Oh, Rob, I'm so sorry!"

Rob's gaze was locked on David. "Some buddy you are!" he challenged fiercely. "One minute you're spouting God and Holy Joe religion, the next you're cutting me to pieces! Man, who needs it?"

Eva pushed her chair back hastily and went to Rob, offering a consoling embrace. "David didn't mean anything wrong, darling. He cares about you. We all care—"

Rob clenched his fists and jerked his arms outward, severing the caress and propelling Eva back against David's chair. "Leave me alone!" he shrieked. "Stop coddling me—telling me everything will be okay! All of you, just give me breathing space!" He wheeled around and retreated down the hall to his room, slamming the door with a violent shudder.

For several interminable seconds, deadening stillness hovered like low-hanging smog, suffocating, strangling us. Eva stood motionless, clinging to the back of David's chair, her knuckles white, her face ashen. Finally, her delicate nostrils flared as she sucked for air, for relief. There was none.

Before any of us could reach out to her, an uproar erupted in Rob's room, ear-splitting pandemonium—thuds, bangs, a resounding clattering—as though Rob were tearing the room apart pillar by post. The noise set us in motion at once. We raced down the hall, pushing against one another in our effort to reach Rob.

Eva threw open his door, then froze, panic-stricken. Rob was swinging his cane wildly, knocking pictures and trophies from the dresser. Coins and books tumbled. His Navy photograph crashed, the glass shattering. He reached up with a violent thrust and dashed his model airplanes to the floor, crushing one with his foot. A torrent of words followed. "Oh, God—oh, God, help me!" he agonized. "I'm still a prisoner. Still a prisoner!"

Pam broke away from us and ran to Rob. "Rob," she said quietly, "give me the cane."

He balked, shaking his head, lifting the cane defiantly.

She closed in on him, holding out her hand. For a moment I was afraid he would swing at her. Then he seemed to crumple inwardly. He lowered his arms and leaned against the cane, his shoulders hunched forward, like a wizened, weary old man. "I'm okay, Pam. I'm just angry," he said tonelessly.

"I know," she said gently. "It's okay, Rob. Let it all out."

I stared at the destruction around us and wondered how Pam could tell him so calmly that it was all right.

David stayed by Eva's side, holding her arm protectively. Clearly stunned by Rob's outburst, she bent slowly and picked up the broken swimming trophy and placed it on the dresser. "This was my son's," she said in anguish. "The son I remember."

Rob was rigid again, his cane raised defensively. "I can never be that son. I've told you a thousand times. I'm not Rob Thornton. I'm Cory Rugby!" He glared lividly at David. "Did you hear that, Dave? Cory Rugby. You got a sermon for Rugby?"

"None," David said contritely. "I blew the last one."

Rob stooped down to retrieve the crumpled plane, its right wing broken, dangling. He studied it with a curious fascination. "These are yesterday's toys," he muttered. "Who needs them?"

"I need them," Eva answered stoutly.

He thrust the plane at Eva. "Here, keep your memories. I have my own to live with." The cutting bitterness in his voice sliced through the room like a saber. He reached up and tore the one remaining plane from the ceiling. Mockingly he swooped it through the air with boyish zeal, then viciously flung it into the wastebasket. "I should have died in that crash in Nam, huh, Dave?"

Eva backed off, swaying unsteadily, cradling the crushed plane in her arms. "Don't ever say that, Rob. Whatever I have done wrong—whatever I've done to you, I'm sorry. But I love you, son."

His eyes met hers like hot coals burning through her, derisive, defying. "Love?" he challenged. "You're smothering me with your endless questions, your cookie-cutter mold of the old Rob!" He rubbed his hands over his cane as if he were shaping clay. "No more," he screamed. "Don't tell me about love or God or your precious memories!" He waved his cane like a rod of protection. "Just keep your distance. All of you!"

He surveyed us, his eyes lingering momentarily, yearningly on me. Then, his emotions spent, he turned to the window. Pressing his forehead against the pane, he trembled involuntarily. His voice breaking, he said, "I don't deserve your love, Mom."

Was he crying? I wondered. Would he turn violent again? Did he really want us not to love him? I looked helplessly at Eva. She was watching her son, still clinging to his model plane, but I couldn't mistake the mixture of pain and fear in her eyes. Yes, it was true. Eva was afraid of her own son.

I ached for her. Rob might never be well, really well. The terrible secret that he held inside was destroying him. For one rending, excruciating moment I wondered, *Oh, God, would it have been better for Eva if Rob had remained dead, still idolized in his mother's eyes?*

CHAPTER
FIFTEEN

On Sunday the fragrance of a dozen red roses greeted Eva and me when we returned from church. For a moment I hoped they were a peace offering from David; he had seemed so remote during the service.

Eva examined the card and exclaimed, "Why, they're for me!"

"From Commander Thomas? He's certainly been attentive lately."

"No, Michelle, they're from my son. He says, 'I'm sorry for the outburst yesterday. Forgive me. We both need to be free of Rob.' "

"He signed it Cory Rugby," I noted, shaking my head somberly.

"He may have signed it Cory, but it's Rob's handwriting." Eva's eyes misted. "The last time Rob sent me roses was the night before he went overseas. He promised me then he'd come home again."

I leaned down and breathed in the freshness of the roses. Rob may have promised to come home,

I mused silently, but not in another man's image, with another man's name. Eva hadn't bargained on that.

Still, she was magnificently resilient. Rob could reject her, lash out at her, hold her at bay, but he couldn't stop her from loving him—as long as loving Rob didn't destroy Eva! Or me.

All week long, as I gazed at Eva's delicate, fading flowers, I thought about Rob's desperate inner struggle and the unexpected, pivotal role I found myself playing in his battle for self-identity. I thought about David and the unspoken breech between us. I agreed to return to the office on Tuesdays and Thursdays—a partial concession to David that resulted in a flimsy, uneasy truce. But in spite of David's disapproval I staunchly refused to give up driving Rob to San Diego for his counseling sessions.

As the early days of March slipped by, I realized David and I would have to talk. Lately, I was constantly analyzing our relationship, fretting over the discord between us, and wondering whether we were making a mistake to plan a life together. I knew I loved David, would always love him, but marriage would have to be based on more than our emotional involvement or even simply caring for each other. David was a strong, decisive, self-assured man whose integrity and dependability made me feel safe, secure, willing to trust my life to him. He made me feel wanted, needed. He had won not only my love, but also my respect and admiration—unlike Scott, for whom I had felt only a passionate, unrealistic abandonment, but never genuine trust.

But for all his good qualities, David could also be domineering, unreasonable, narrow, and unbending. I was independent, too, and self-willed. Somehow I had to figure out how to be true to myself, to David, and to God. Was I expected to give up my own personhood—my writing, my zeal, my castle-dreams—to a man?

Finally, while David was away on a three-day business trip, I snatched every opportunity to be alone, to escape from Pam's endless prattle about the incomparable Lance Edwards, and to avoid Rob's sullen eyes following my every move—away from the arduous claims of the Thornton household. I wanted God's answer, God's direction in my life. His alone. I wanted a marriage that would please Him. I knew that a Christ-honoring marriage would require a blending of our personalities, a unity of purpose, and perhaps, hardest for me to imagine, submission to my husband's authority. With my impulsive, creative, stubborn nature, could I actually defer to David's judgment in every aspect of my life? Would it mean giving up the book I was writing, the strides I had made with Rob? But even as I raised these questions, I feared that God might take David out of my life, leaving me bitter and empty.

I went back to Laguna Beach to the boulder-strewn cliff, a sheer, deserted bluff jutting out over the ocean. I dropped down on the grassy cove. The surf raged, my heart pounded. The chill, salty breeze caught my tears. I cried and prayed and remembered how beautiful it had been to be here with David. It was here that he had told me he loved me. As the spumy waves washed in, spraying, splashing, shattering my feeble attempts to bargain with God, I knew that I would always love David. I loved him enough to give him up.

On the Tuesday after David returned from his

business trip, I asked him to drive me home from work.

He looked quizzical. "Your Honda's not working?"

"Yes, but I rode with Eva. I wanted you and me to talk—privately."

"It sounds serious," he said as we walked to his car.

I nodded. I felt small, fragile beside David, vulnerable to the crisp spring wind, and to the stark, raw emotions assailing me now. I had never loved David more.

"I missed you," he said as we settled in the car. "I thought about you the whole time I was gone."

"Me, too," I whispered back.

"But something's wrong?"

"Not with you, David." I fidgeted absently with my watchband. "I rehearsed this a thousand times, and now—now I don't know how to tell you."

David took a firm grip on the wheel, his body tensing beside me. "Tell me what, Michelle?"

"David, I love you."

He relaxed slightly. "You rehearsed that a thousand times? Is it so hard to say?" There was a controlled anxiety in his tone.

"No, it's not. It's just—I don't know if you'll understand but I—I've got to surrender my claims to you—"

He glanced over, raising one eyebrow. "What kind of double-talk is that?"

"It's the truth, David. I have to let you go."

David swerved over to the curb and braked abruptly. He turned off the engine and faced me, his expression jarringly distorted, the shock in his eyes devastating me. "Who is it, Michelle? Rob?"

"There's no one else. Certainly not Rob."

"Then what? Why? You just said you love me."

With a breathless rush of words, I stammered, "It's not what you think, David. There could never be anyone else for me. I just—I don't know if I could be a good wife—submissive, obedient. God showed me—convicted me—"

"I never asked you to obey me. We're not even married yet."

"But you told me I must stop driving Rob—and you don't approve of the book I'm writing—and we hardly talk anymore. We're not walking together in the same direction. We're tugging against each other. We can't please God that way."

David reached out for me, his hand caressing my shoulder, my hair. "Have I driven you away? Michelle, you can't do this—"

"It's not me, David. I—I have to be available to Rob. I'm committed to his recovery."

"So am I. But Rob's recovery has nothing to do with us."

"But it does. Rob depends on me, trusts no one else. Yet you want me to stop driving him to San Diego. Don't you see, David? I'm torn between helping Rob and complying with your wishes. As long as we're promised to each other, I feel I can't disobey you. So I have no choice but to free you and obey the dictates of my own heart."

"Is that what you think God wants for us?" David challenged.

My throat locked. "For now—yes."

"So Rob and his book mean more to you than I do?"

"That's not fair, David! This is the hardest thing I've ever had to do." My voice sounded thin and shrill, like a fine wire pulled taut. "When I lost Scott,

I was bitter and angry against God. I never thought I'd get over it. But now I've learned—in fact, you've taught me so much, David—the importance of listening to God, doing His will. He's given me a new joy in Him, David. I—I no longer feel like a spiritual novice next to you. That's why I've got to do this, David—" My words were fractured, faltering. "That's why I've got to . . . break our engagement."

"Then that's it? It's final?" David didn't wait for my answer but swiveled around in his seat, stiffening, drawing away from me physically and emotionally. I felt the wall rise between us with a swift, acute pang.

David started the engine and drove the few blocks to Eva's condo in desolate, ice-cutting silence. I thought of a hundred ways to tell him I was sorry, but the words died in my throat. My mouth felt parched, coated with cotton. Nausea started in the pit of my stomach and churned upward.

David parked and escorted me to the door with a brisk formality. When I dared to steal a glance his way, his expression was stricken, doleful, the scar on his chin white with barely repressed fury.

"Would you like to come in?" I ventured weakly.

In a mute gesture of deep pain David touched my cheek, his gaze searing, then wheeled around sharply and stalked back to his car.

For the next two weeks David and I exchanged only the polite, abbreviated conversation of nodding acquaintances. His remarks were always clipped, contained, his gaze focused somewhere beyond me. At work I avoided him, which wasn't difficult since he also avoided me. He stopped dropping by Eva's and telephoned only to discuss business matters. I pretended that our breakup was not a life-shattering event for me, but I walked around shaken, stunned, with an ache in my chest like a constant, unrelieved sob.

I continued to drive Rob to San Diego three days a week for his counseling sessions. For the first time since I'd known him, Rob's spirits seemed almost buoyant. He talked freely to me now, sharing every detail wrenched from the shadows of his memory by his psychiatrist. Every session was grueling, draining. Increasingly Rob balked against going. "Can't I just talk to you, Michelle?" he asked after one troubling session as we strolled through the Spanish courtyard between the hospital's salmon-pink buildings. "The doctors are like clumsy dentists drilling into exposed nerve endings."

"They're doing their job, Rob," I reminded him. "Maybe it has to get worse before it can get better."

"You mean I've got to feel the pain before I'm purged?"

"I don't know, Rob." We followed the circular brick walkway around the center fountain area and sat down on a tile bench. The pond was brimming with lily pads, and a jet of water spouted from a chubby ceramic cherub. "Did you remember something new today?"

"The prison camps," Rob mumbled, his gaze downcast.

"Do you want to tell me?" I asked gently.

His gaze drifted to the old-fashioned fire escape—a dark, spidery appendage on the timeworn stucco building. "I remember the numbing, suffocating monotony," he murmured, "and the stench of open sewers on muggy nights. I remember the cockroaches and rats running freer than we were. Sometimes even with 100 percent humidity the only place it rained was inside our clothes." He choked back a low, guttural sound. "I remember ragtag guys turning into walking, hallucinating skeletons, and I can see red blood spilled out on green fields."

"Rob, you don't have to go on," I told him.

"Yes, I do," he said fiercely. "They want me to remember. So I will. I can still hear the squawky speaker droning Communist propaganda into my prison cell hour after hour after hour. I remember the reeducation camps—hoeing the rice paddies until I dropped, then the muzzle of a gun in my ribs forcing me up again. I recall the dysentery, the exhaustion, the unrelieved hunger pangs. My feet were cracked open, my hands raw hamburger, my face a mass of welts from mosquitoes. But the worst part, the most defiling, despicable—" He paused, the vision behind his eyes apparently too harrowing to verbalize. His hand moved nervously, his index finger tracing invisible numbers on the tile bench. "The worst thing was the unrestrained savagery— the torture, the shame and humiliation, the utter degradation—"

"Rob, please, don't—"

"They stripped us naked, hung us on poles over a crossbeam, tied our hands behind us, and stretched us until our shoulders were pulled from their sockets." Rob's voice throbbed with emotion. "Once they took me out and made me dig my own grave. They made me kneel, beg for my life. I wept like a baby. Then they fired a gun beside my head. The blast echoed through my senses like an electric shock. It took a full minute before I realized I wasn't dead. They had deliberately missed."

"Rob, what about your friends—the other men? Do you remember them—who they were?"

"They're still shadows, Michelle, their faces a blur. I know in the POW camps we were constantly trying to communicate. It was all we had. The guards kept telling us we were alone, that no one knew we were there, no one cared. But we had this code worked out. We tapped messages between our cells. We listened with our tin cups pressed against the concrete walls. We memorized the names of every man in the camp—everyone who arrived, everyone who died, so someday one of us could get out and tell someone back home. Only now, God help me, I can't remember the names or the faces—almost no one, except Cory Rugby." He sucked in an angry breath. "And now, blasted irony, no one here at home even believes I am Cory Rugby!"

"Rob, try to look at the positive side. You do recall everything since you escaped to Laos—your four years with the Hmong people."

His expression softened, his eyes glistened. "It's strange, Michelle. Some parts of my mind have been dead for years, but other parts were awakened vibrantly in Laos. I became attuned to the fresh, green smells of the countryside, the brilliance of the evening sky, and—and the softness of Liana's skin beside me in the night. She kept me going, Michelle, gave me a reason to be alive when I thought there was nothing left of my own world. You see, I didn't even know if there was an America to go home to. Saigon had fallen. No one had come to rescue me, and I vaguely recalled the guards showing me photos of a Communist flag flying over the Capitol in Washington."

"Oh, Rob, it had to be trick photography!" I exclaimed.

"I know that now." He was still unconsciously

tracing the same sequence of numbers on the bench.

"Rob, you keep tracing numbers over and over. You don't even realize you're doing it. Could they mean something?"

"I don't know—they're just there in my mind."

"They're not your Navy I.D.?"

"My dog tag number? No." He was certain of that.

"Your Social Security?"

He whipped out his wallet, then heaved a sigh. "Not even close."

"A phone number perhaps?"

"Too many numbers. . .unless I have a girlfriend in Europe." His faint attempt at humor fell flat as he stood, his shoulders sagging dejectedly. "Let's forget the numbers. They're not important."

Rob might forget them, but I couldn't. Inside, a nagging, nebulous uncertainty, an obscure possibility tantalized me. With all that Rob had just shared, I was convinced that he teetered between finding himself and staggering over the brink of insanity. I was desperate to help him solve the enigma of Cory Rugby. Could the mysterious numbers help?

The possibilities kept tumbling through my head all the way home to Irvine. Were the numbers a zip code? An old phone listing? Could it be as simple as that—a girlfriend's phone number—Tammy Marlor, Rob's old college sweetheart who kept in touch with Eva at Christmastime? The Thorntons' home phone back in Indiana? Or worse, Rob's prison number? Did they have them? He had never said.

When we reached the house, I asked Rob to jot down the numbers in my writer's notebook. I went to my room and sat at my desk, studying them. Ten numbers: 5155554356. It could be a phone number with the area code. On impulse—before I changed my mind—I reached for the phone, dialed, and asked for directory assistance.

Unable to quell my mounting excitement, I told the operator I needed to trace a number. In a singsong monotone she said, "That number is in Winterset, Iowa. Would you like me to dial for you?"

"No, I'll dial myself. Thank you." I slipped the phone back into its cradle, thinking, *So it wasn't Rob's old hometown. Then what? Did I have the nerve?* I picked up the phone again and dialed.

On the second ring I almost hung up, but deep, gnawing curiosity propelled me on. Three—five—ten rings. I waited. Finally, on the twelfth ring, a gruff voice answered, "Rugby's residence."

I caught my breath. "Mr. Rugby?" I ventured.

"Colonel Rugby," he corrected. "How can I help you?"

"I'm calling for a friend." I paused. "A friend of your son's."

A deadening silence followed. Then a crusty, pain-filled voice cut across the wires from Winterset to Irvine. "Is this some sort of joke?"

"Sir, I'm sorry. I—it's just—"

"Who are you?" he demanded. "Why are you calling like this?"

"I'm Michelle Merrill," I answered softly, hating myself for inflicting the wound that would fester if this was indeed Cory Rugby's father. "I need to find out about Cory Rugby," I told him.

"You're twelve years too late."

"Please, listen," I stammered. "A friend of mine may have known your son in Vietnam."

"I have no son," he uttered scathingly. Before I could respond, the phone went dead.

I'd blown it. My first real clue to Cory Rugby, and

I had rushed in blindly. The muscles in my neck and shoulders tightened. A sickening headache clamped against my skull. As I sat rubbing my forehead, the words of the local librarian came back to me: "Unless you know the young man's hometown...the librarian there...newspaper stacks ...court records...."

I glanced at my watch. There was still time before Eva and Pam arrived to make another call. I forced myself to stay calm. When the gentle-voiced librarian at the Winterset Library answered, my words ran together as I told her my story, Rob's story. Something in my desperate cry for help struck a responsive chord. "How can I help?" she offered.

"I'm baffled," I admitted. "Colonel Rugby said he had no son."

"Oh, that's the old man's line. Colonel Rugby, I mean. Actually, he had two sons."

"Then why would he tell me he had none?"

"Humph! I'm certain there were two sons. The Rugbys have lived here for years.... The boys grew up here...their names? Collin, I think. And Larry or Lonnie, something like that."

"Not Cory?"

"Yes, come to think of it. It was Cory. They have a plaque in his honor in one of the parks. Yes, the Colonel definitely had two sons. One burned his draft card and the other went off to war."

"You're sure?" My palms were moist, my pulse racing.

"Of course. It made headlines here in Winterset."

"But why would the Colonel tell me he had no sons?"

"Colonel Rugby's all Army, a career man," the librarian replied. "He considered a man who wouldn't go to war a coward, so he felt personally disgraced when one of his boys refused to go. And what's worse—poor blind man, him playing religious and all, he just couldn't accept that a son of his would be captured, taken prisoner in Vietnam. Just before the war ended, too. The boy's still listed as an MIA. But the Colonel pretends he never existed."

"What happened to Cory's brother?"

"Nobody knows, though I suppose someone down at the drug store might know. It's kind of a favorite gathering place here in Winterset. But I don't think that son ever came back home either. He wouldn't be welcome at the Rugby farm, that's for sure. Maybe the missus would forgive him—poor woman—but not Colonel Rugby."

"I was wondering," I said, before hanging up, "do you think you could check in the newspaper stacks for old articles on the Rugby boys?"

"I think I could do that for you," she promised, the intrigue evidently appealing to her. "I'll see what I can find and send copies right out to you."

Shortly after I hung up the telephone, I heard someone knocking at the front door. I hurried to answer it, murmuring, "Eva, I bet you forgot your key..."

I opened the door and stared up in mute surprise at David.

"Hello, Michelle," he said politely. "How are you?"

"Fine. Fine. Never better," I blurted. I touched my hair and wondered whether my makeup was still fresh. "I'm sorry, David. Eva isn't here—"

"I know," he said quietly. "I just left her at the office. I came to see you."

"Oh, I see. I mean, I *don't* see—"

"I tried telephoning you, but the line was busy—"

"Yes, I was calling...someone."

"So on impulse I decided to drive over."

"You didn't have to, David."

"Yes. Yes, I did. We have to talk, Michelle."

I stepped back from the doorway, shaking my head, puzzled. "We've already said everything—"

"No. You've said everything perhaps, but not me. I've got something I need to tell you, Michelle."

I turned and walked to the living room. David followed. I sat on the sofa; he took the desk chair and swiveled to face me. I cleared my throat nervously. "You know, David, rehashing everything won't help. It'll only make things worse."

"I'm not rehashing—"

"I haven't changed my mind about driving Rob to San Diego."

"I'm not asking you to, Michelle."

"Are you saying you've changed *your* mind?"

David raised his hands in a mildly protesting gesture. "No, Michelle. I still feel the same. But I've realized something important. I have a tendency to make decisions for other people, to take charge of their lives, and that's not right. No matter how I feel about it, the time you spend with Rob has to be your own choice—just as I have to respect your decision to...to end our relationship." His eyes met mine directly. "Only time will tell whether your decision was right for us."

"Thank you for admitting that, David," I said, lowering my gaze.

"I'm not finished, Michelle." He straightened his shirt cuff although it was already starched and bone-stiff. He looked immaculate, as always. "I want you to know, Michelle—I've struggled with this. I've been angry—and I don't like feeling out of control. You already know—"

"I know, David. I'm sorry. I never meant to hurt you."

"That's not what I'm getting at, Michelle." He stood and walked over to the window. "The last time we talked—when you said good-bye, I felt—such rage. Irrational. I wanted to strike out. I wanted to hurt you—not physically. Emotionally."

I felt tears sting my eyes. "Oh, David, please don't talk about it—"

He pivoted and approached the sofa. "Listen, Michelle, I've got to say this now while I've got the words. I don't mind telling you, these past two weeks I've faced the greatest spiritual battle of my life since my days in Nam. I've wrestled with myself—and God." His voice splintered. "I know now that I—I've got to free you, Michelle."

A sob tore at my throat. "Free me?"

David leaned down and touched my chin lightly. "We can't go our separate ways or make new lives for ourselves as long as there's this—this animosity between us." His eyes moistened. "I want us to be friends, Michelle. I'm not saying I'll ever be able to think of you just as a friend, but I do know that God wants me to be willing to let you go . . . without bitterness . . . without question." He took my hand and raised it to his lips. "I free you, darling. I wish you the very—"

I pressed David's hand against my cheek. "Oh, David, I'm not sure it wasn't easier before, when I knew you were angry with me. I can deal with your anger—but not your love, your integrity!"

David slowly withdrew his hand and straightened

his shoulders. "I'd better go, Michelle. There's just one more thing."

I stood up and walked him to the door. "What is it, David?"

Taking both my hands in his, he said, "I want you to know I believe in your writing, in your skills and commitment. It's just that I can't share your dream when it comes to Rob's story."

"Oh, David, I wish you could understand. I wish you could see how my writing has taken on new discipline and dimension since I've begun this project. It's no longer a matter of writing for writing's sake but of using my talent to make others aware of human need. Don't you see, David? I feel as if God is channeling me in new and exciting directions."

David's expression clouded. His hands still gripped mine, almost too tightly. His dark eyes burned into mine with a fiery intensity. "No matter what you say about the book, Michelle, I'm convinced you're treading on dangerous ground. Rob's past is buried in the depths of Southeast Asia. By digging into his history, you may uncover secrets that will only defraud Rob's memory and perhaps even destroy his chance for recovery."

Reflectively I murmured, "I'm not sure anyone can unlock Rob's past. His secrets are as shadowy, as elusive as the East wind."

"What did you say, Michelle?"

"Nothing, really, David. Nothing I can explain."

With crisp efficiency he released my hands and opened the door. "Friends?" he asked.

I gave a quick nod of my head.

He reached out and cupped my face in his palms, then gently kissed my forehead. "I'll never stop loving you, Michelle. Perhaps someday when this is all over, we'll find each other again. But no matter what happens, we've invested too much in each other to forfeit our friendship."

"I feel that way too, David," I said wistfully.

He stepped outside and looked back at me for a long minute. A fragrant spring breeze turned his cheeks ruddy and ruffled his hair, giving his face a sad, boyish vulnerability. I wanted to run into his arms and comfort him and never let him go.

"I do love you, David," I cried, gripping the doorpost with a resolute fierceness lest I leap into his embrace.

He managed a tight, grimacing smile. "For my stubbornness?"

"For yourself," I whispered tearfully.

CHAPTER
SIXTEEN

The following Tuesday I was back at the office with David's words *I'll never stop loving you, Michelle...perhaps someday* ringing, running, dancing in my heart and mind. We were friends again. It wasn't his magical touch or those wonderful, whimsical whisperings of love in my ear, but at least we were talking again. Really talking. And although at times I longed to be held in his arms, we were stepping back, taking a good long look at each other, discovering qualities of friendship that our fast-paced romance hadn't permitted.

Even the thought that David and I might never marry could not completely dim the inner peace I felt. I loved David more than ever—for his integrity and humility, his brokenness and his willingness to trust God with the outcome of our relationship.

But, of course, there was still the issue of Rob. It was David's sense of justice that gnawed at him in his dealings with Rob. He questioned Rob's motives, pondered over Rob's lost years. Now I wanted to solve the elusive mystery of Cory Rugby as much for David as for Rob. But Rob wasn't making it any easier.

"Do you plan to dream all day?" Mitzi Piltz's silky voice startled me. She was sitting across from my desk, studying me with her shrewd, calculating green eyes, one penciled eyebrow arched quizzically.

"Good morning, Mitzi," I greeted.

"Looks like some of us get paid for working for Mr. Ballard and some of us get paid just to *think* about him."

A mixture of fury and embarrassment colored my cheeks. "I had my mind on something, Mitzi."

"Obviously," she said, looking half-amused. "Or was it *someone*?"

I glanced immediately toward David's office and heard Mitzi's tantalizing chuckle as his door opened. David emerged and caught my eye at once, giving me a quick, almost indiscernible wink. Then he crooked his finger, beckoning me to him.

From the corner of my eye I noticed Mitzi's fingers fluttering in return. For a moment I thought she would get up and go to him, but she sheepishly eased back into her chair. "I believe Mr. Ballard wants *you*," she said, her irritation mounting.

"Sorry, Michelle," David murmured as I approached. "I just didn't want Mitzi to overhear us." He paused meaningfully. "I just talked with Commander Thomas."

"He called?"

"No. Actually I called him to ask him to speak at the Men's Fellowship Breakfast in May. While we were talking, he told me about Rob skipping his psychiatric appointment."

"Oh, David, I should have told you. I just didn't want to upset you—not when...."

"It's okay, Michelle. It's not your fault." David's gaze reached out tenderly to me. His voice was low, constrained. "Frankly, the Commander advises hospitalization. He told Eva that with Rob's outbursts and potential for violence, he could be a threat to himself—or others."

"Really, David! I feel perfectly safe with Rob."

He tweaked my cheek playfully. "My sweet little naive Michelle. You're so trusting. So loyal. But promise me you'll be careful."

"I'm always careful, David. But the point is, for Rob, being cooped up in the hospital would be like—like being back in prison."

"Not according to the Commander. If Rob went back as an inpatient, they'd have him on active duty at least half a day—training in electronics or working in the office. He'd be busy."

"You could give him a job here."

"I offered. He wants no part of Ballard Computer Design. He said Eva and I just want to keep an eye on him."

"Well, at least you tried, David."

"Michelle, one more thing—" He looked apologetic. "Commander Thomas assured Eva that if Rob cuts one more appointment, hospitalization will no longer be an option. It'll be an order."

I went back to my desk, feeling Mitzi's curious gaze following my every step. I had told David that I felt perfectly safe with Rob. But did I? Could David be right? Was I risking my own safety? How many times had I heard Rob saying, *I killed someone*?

Had he? Was he really capable of murder? Had

I been wrong in not sharing Rob's alarming confidence with David? *Sweet little naive Michelle.*

I gave Mitzi a quick nod, more grimace than smile, sat down at my desk and rolled a sheet of paper into my typewriter, willing myself to concentrate on the work at hand. *But when I get home tonight*, I promised myself, *I'll spread out Rob's manuscript file.* I had to find the answer to Cory Rubgy. The missing link was there somewhere . . . somewhere in the scattered bits and pieces of Rob's life that were slowly coming together in the rough draft of his story. I already had a possible title: *Rob Thornton: A Vietnam Legacy.*

A week later, the second Wednesday in April, Rob and I arrived home early from San Diego. For the second time in two weeks, he had stubbornly refused to keep his psychiatric appointment at the Naval Hospital. In grudging silence I curled up on the sofa, trying to concentrate on the day's mail, vainly attempting to cool my growing impatience with Rob. Even discovering the librarian's letter from Winterset didn't buoy me up. I wasn't looking forward to telling David or Eva what had happened. I might not have to. By now Commander Thomas may have phoned the office and informed them of Rob's absence. At any moment, David or Eva might burst in through the front door, David's concern mushrooming, Eva no longer free to delay Rob's return to the hospital.

If that happened all the strides I had made with Rob were destined for failure. I wanted to go over and shake and scold him like a little boy, but today it was impossible to reason with him. Rob's back was to me. He was playing the piano obsessively, with relentless energy, the decades-old melodies burning inside of him.

I looked back at the letter in my hands. The librarian in Winterset had kept her word. She had enclosed three articles on the Rugbys. A small social column noted, COLONEL RUGBY RETIRES IN WINTERSET. A front page clipping proclaimed darkly, RUGBY SON MISSING IN ACTION. And the oldest of the three articles blazed, THE WOUNDS OF WAR: A FAMILY DIVIDED. The opening sentence caught my attention: "Once again Vietnam divides a family as it claims the Rugbys of Winterset." The accompanying newpaper photos of the Rugby boys revealed blurred silhouettes—a proud young man in Marine uniform and the side view of his younger brother burning his draft card. There wasn't even a vague similarity between the faded photographs and Rob Thornton.

I found myself rereading the lines, puzzling over how they could possibly relate to Rob. As I debated on sharing them with him, the front doorbell rang.

Rob finished a note or two of a Broadway tune, then swung around on the piano bench. "I'll get it."

Moments later he was back. "It's Lance Edwards, Michelle. He wants to see you."

Lance had already entered the room, his visor cap in hand, as he brushed his unruly wheat-brown hair into place. "Good afternoon, Michelle."

I groaned inwardly. "I thought we were finally rid of you, Lance," I bantered ruefully as I tucked the Winterset clippings back in the envelope. "I figured Pam had come to her senses—you haven't been around for days."

"Five days to be exact," he answered, obviously thriving on our continuing private rivalry. "Aren't you going to ask me where I've been?"

"Tell me."

"Back in Iowa."

"Iowa?" I echoed, my pulse racing. *Winterset, Iowa?* I wondered. *Had Pam found the Rugby phone number and given it to Lance? Had Lance had the audacity to visit the Rugbys?*

"You look rather discomfited," he challenged. "Did Iowa strike a familiar chord?"

"Why should it?"

"We're both looking for the same answers, aren't we?"

"Answers?" I said numbly. Should I pursue it? Did I dare admit here in front of Rob that I had called Winterset? That I knew where Cory Rugby had lived?

"I thought you might be checking out things for the maestro over there." Lance nodded at Rob who sat at the piano scowling back at us.

"You went too far west, Edwards," Rob said. "The Thorntons are from Indiana."

"I'm not looking for answers in Indiana," Lance answered cockily.

There was a flicker of interest in Rob's eyes.

Lance pressed his point. "I was out at old Winterset High." He paused. Was he waiting for Rob's reaction? I couldn't be sure.

"Winterset?" Rob mulled the word over.

"A quaint little town in Iowa. I did a bit of work at the news office and in the musty stacks at the library." Lance shot a glance my way, his lips coiled. "They told me someone else was interested in the old stories. Football hero joins Marines. Helicopter pilot down in Vietnam. Rugby missing in action." He glared at Rob. "Or do you suppose he was *killed* in Indochina?"

"I think you'd better go, Lance," I said uneasily, glancing at Rob. I didn't like Rob's nervous facial twitch, that vacant, haunted look in his eyes when he was remembering.

"What are you trying to do, man?" Rob asked, on his feet now, his fists doubling. "What are you trying to do to me?"

"I keep wondering what your game is," returned Lance. "Amnesia? Could be." His tone was cutting, sarcastic. "Or some secret sin buried in Southeast Asia?"

Rob lunged for Lance. I stepped between them. "Get out of here, Lance. Go before Eva gets here and sees what you're doing to Rob." Impulsively I shoved Lance. His rock-hard chest was like a granite barrier. He didn't budge.

Lance looked at me with bemused disdain. "You're a puzzlement to me, Miss Merrill. You're so busy protecting your hero, researching your manuscript, that you miss what's right under your nose." His tone was caustic. "Don't worry, I won't interfere with your book."

I felt confused, almost faint. All I wanted was Lance Edwards out of the house before Eva got home.

"Whether you want to face it or not, I'm going to find out what makes your Navy boy tick." Lance's upper lip curled in a sneer. "So he says he doesn't remember. How convenient. He mopes around here feeling sorry for himself. But at least he lived through the war, didn't he?"

Rob's body went rigid. "So where were you during the war, Edwards?" he screamed out.

"In Canada, man. Where you should have been."

"So you ran out?"

"I didn't want to spill my guts in Vietnam. I wanted to be a journalist." Lance paused, breathless. "I was too young, too inexperienced to be a war correspondent."

"They died too," growled Rob. "Some of them. The Viet Cong couldn't tell the difference between a newsman and a soldier."

"See what I mean? Their lives were wasted," Lance uttered bitterly. "Every man who died over there. Wasted!"

"You're nothing but a dirty, stinking, yellow coward!" shouted Rob. "What did you do—burn your draft card and run like blazes?"

"Stop it, Rob!" I demanded. "You're just getting yourself upset. Lance Edwards isn't worth it."

"She's right, Lt. Thornton. That's what my family said—I'm not worth it."

Until this moment I had held little more than contempt for Lance Edwards—his constant prying, his cockiness. Now as I stared helplessly at the two men, I pitied them both. Rob struggling to find himself. Lance on the run, rejected by his own family.

Rob glared at us both, then pivoted and stalked from the room.

Lance shouted after him, "That's it, Lieutenant, run yourself! Every time you get close to remembering, you run. *You're* the stinking, yellow coward!"

Rob whirled around and froze in the hallway. "Call me a coward, will you? You . . . get out. Just get out!"

When Rob had limped off to his room, I turned to Lance and said, "Do as Rob says. Leave him alone.

We're trying to help him get well. You're just going to destroy every gain we've made."

Lance took a handkerchief from his jacket pocket and mopped his forehead. The brash, self-assured Lance Edwards was ashen. Sweat poured down his face, dripping into the loose-fitting collar of his striped shirt. He reached up and loosened his tie. The vein in his neck pulsated.

"I don't understand," I said as I walked Lance to the door. "You're so involved in the MIA/POW issue. Yet you obviously had no allegiance to the war itself."

"The war was stupid," he snarled.

"Fighting for freedom is never stupid," I countered hotly.

"It was a good way to get killed. That's why I went to Canada."

There it was again. His escape route. "Were you there the whole war?"

"I went as an eighteen-year-old kid. I never came back until the President offered us amnesty. I'm not proud of it." He shrugged. "Like I said, I just didn't want to get killed in a rotten war."

"No one does."

"But I did something about it."

"Ran?" I challenged, repeating Rob's question.

Lance paused in the hallway. "I guess I didn't see it as running. I wanted to live so badly. Actually I had relatives in Canada. An uncle. I worked his farm in Calgary for years. He sent me to college."

"And you majored in journalism."

Lance's presumptuous smirk was back. "Yeah." He shifted, twirling his visor cap. "You know, I might have missed Vietnam, but—"

"I know you did." I opened the door for him.

Lance Edwards was no longer in a hurry. "Michelle, I know you don't like me. You think I'm a callused, overbearing bully. But I'll tell you this. I've had a war of my own. The President gave me unconditional amnesty, but my family didn't. Except for my uncle, they've barely spoken to me since I was eighteen years old."

I felt a ripple of sympathy for him. "I'm sorry, Lance."

"I didn't say it for pity." Lance's voice was tinged with irony. "I missed my war, got my journalism degree, and lost my family. But I determined that I would earn my reputation as a writer. And I'm good, decidedly good. When I came back from Canada, there were no flags waving, no welcome mats. I didn't go through the living hell that Rob Thornton has experienced. But I've had my own prison. I guess that's why I follow every MIA and POW lead I hear about in this country. I figure that way I can make up a little for my cowardice."

I shivered in the open doorway, chilled by the brisk April air and the obvious pain Lance was feeling. Lance Edwards could spend his whole lifetime mending his ways, trying to redeem himself. For the first time since meeting him, I realized that Lance needed a Redeemer. The man annoyed me. We had clashed on numerous occasions and locked words time and again. He angered me. At times he was repulsive. But I was so busy disliking him that I had forgotten that Jesus loved him. I stammered for words, "Lance, Jesus cares about you. He can forgive—"

Lance held up his cap like a big stop sign. "If y 're going to preach, don't. I've been around long enough to know that this is a God-house."

I didn't like his description.

"You know—religious and all."

"Not religious," I protested.

He licked his dry lips. "I know. Rob Thornton is lucky. He's got a family with a faith in God big enough to love him and want him well. And God help us, he's hard enough to love."

Lance slapped his cap on his head and tipped the visor to me. "Have a good day, Michelle—even though I didn't contribute much to it." He vacillated on the porch, looking thoughtful. "There's a story in this house. I've known it since I first knocked on the door. Like any good freelance reporter, I wanted to be the first to write it up. I'm still convinced Rob Thornton is afraid to remember his past."

Only seconds before I had cared for this man's soul—now I was irritated with him again. I started to close the door. He stopped it with his foot. "Go, please," I begged.

He gave me that insolent shrug of his broad shoulders. "By the way, Miss Merrill, I grew up in a God-house. I even hear that my family is still religious. They just don't have any room for me." He turned and was gone with swift, impassioned strides.

I closed the front door tightly, pressed my face against it, and cried.

CHAPTER SEVENTEEN

Shortly after Lance left, I ran to the bathroom and splashed cold water on my tear-stained face. I touched up my makeup so Rob wouldn't know I'd been crying. Then, as I walked toward the kitchen, I noticed that Rob was back at the piano, his hands casually caressing the keys. "Michelle," he said, stopping me. "I think I've seen Edwards before."

"Of course, Rob. Many times. He practically lives here now that he's dating Pam."

"No. Before this." He held his hands poised over the keyboard, then resumed playing the melody of some forgotten song. "I don't think I've ever been in Iowa. But the name . . . Winterset."

His slender fingers moved across the keys with an impressive flourish. Powerful hands. Gentle hands. Scarred hands. I stood behind him watching as he played. I wondered, were those hands strong enough, cruel enough to have killed someone?

"Like it, Michelle?"

"What, Rob?"

"This song I'm playing."

"It sounds familiar."

In his rusty baritone he sang, "... Until the twelfth ... of never ..."

My voice blended with his, finishing with, "... I'll still be loving you ..."

"Will you?" Rob asked wistfully, looking around at me.

"Will I what?"

His eyes clouded. "Will you go with me Saturday?"

"Where?"

"To the cemetery?"

I backed off. "The cemetery?"

He nodded. "Yes. The Riverside National Cemetery. They're having an opening ceremony for the Vietnam Veterans Memorial Wall. Commander Thomas told me about it. He wants me to go."

"I don't understand. That's in Washington, D.C., isn't it?"

"This is a half-size replica that's been on tour through the Western states. It'll only be here a week."

"And you've decided to go? I think that's wonderful, Rob. I'd love to join you."

He hesitated. "There's only one problem. They want me to speak, say a few words. They intend to introduce me as a—a hero." His voice wavered. "For the Commander's sake, I promised I'd be there—but that's all."

Before I could question Rob further, Eva and David arrived. By the look on their faces I was certain they knew Rob had missed his counseling session.

"We've been expecting you," Rob muttered, already defensive. "What took you so long?"

"Commander Thomas called me at work," Eva

said in a softly accusing voice. "Why, Rob?"

"Why? I don't know why he called you."

"Don't you?" David snapped. "Missing your psychiatric appointment again—does that give you a clue?"

Obsessively, in a beating frenzy, Rob pounded out a showy stanza of the Grieg Concerto. Above the echoing, thundering sounds of the piano, he said, "I don't need the doctors any longer. I'm sick of talking about Vietnam."

"But Commander Thomas says—"

"Hang Commander Thomas!" Rob ran the back of his hand up the keyboard, then whirled around on the piano bench.

Eva stood her ground. "Commander Thomas expects you back at the hospital on Monday morning as an inpatient."

"No way. I have other plans."

"Then shelf them," ordered David. "You blew it yourself, man. We didn't break your appointment. You ran out on it."

Rob gave David a scornful, scrutinizing glance. "I bug you, don't I, Dave?"

David glared back. "You really do at times."

"Don't I measure up? The way I see it, you don't have room to talk. After all, from what I hear, you were the one who ran off in Vietnam—not me. You left me to die!"

The muscles in David's face tightened; his color rose. "I've told you before, Rob, the kid threw the grenade. The plane exploded in flames. Where you had been standing, there was nothing. I thought you were dead—blown into a million pieces."

Rob's tone turned venomous. "*You ran!*"

David flinched, his anger smoldering. "Yes," he

admitted. "I ran through that jungle brush after that little almond-eyed boy who tossed the grenade. I wanted to tear out his gut for killing you."

"You *ran*, all right—right back to safety and freedom," countered Rob. "You left me there for the North Vietnamese to find." He spat out the words as savagely as the boy must have hurled his grenade. "Did they give you a hero's medal, Dave? Did they pin ribbons of valor on you for that one?"

Eva sank into the cushion of the nearest chair, stunned, crestfallen. "Rob, David earned his Medal of Honor just like you did. He never did anything to be ashamed of."

"And you're suggesting I *did* do something to be ashamed of?"

"Of course not, Rob. We all know how brave you were."

His voice was heavy with sarcasm. "As brave as Dave here?"

I wanted to shout out, "Tell him, David. Tell him—you were wounded, unconscious, hospitalized yourself." Somehow I couldn't squeeze out the words in David's defense.

But David was ready with an answer. Speaking over crushing anguish, he implored, "Listen to me, Rob. There were no medals for leaving you, but if I could have taken your place—I would have."

No medals, David, I reflected silently, *just a badge of guilt that you've worn all these years for Rob.*

"Take my place, Dave?" Rob mocked. "That's easy for you to say now. But why would you bother? You don't even like me, do you, Dave?"

"*Like* is the wrong word, Rob. I don't *trust* you."

"Because I don't remember everything you expect me to remember?"

"I think you remember more than you let on. Quite a bit more."

"What's that supposed to mean?"

"Interpret it any way you like. But I think you're using us, Rob. Holding on to forgetting—for whatever reason—to protect yourself perhaps. God knows why," David faltered, "I don't."

"Who wants to remember a living hell?" challenged Rob.

"Remembering is the only way back to good health, Rob. You won't get anywhere burying it all inside of you."

Rob fell silent, a tortured expression etched in his face. Finally he whispered, "I buried my friends, Dave. My only friends."

David winced. "We were friends once."

"Were we?" The words wrenched from Rob. There was a distant, tormented glint in his eyes. I sensed that he was no longer here with us in the living room. He was back in Vietnam, in the dense jungle reliving a painful separation from his friends. *I buried my friends*, he said. How did they die? Was Rob somehow responsible? *I killed someone, Michelle*. I trembled.

Rob turned to Eva, holding out his empty hands in a pathetic, childlike gesture, like a youngster with a broken toy. "They were my friends, Mom."

"Who, Rob?" she asked tenderly.

Rob blinked; twitches convulsed his face. "Thornton and Evans."

"You mean *Rugby* and Evans?" David asked quietly, his voice controlled.

Rob focused on David, his faraway gaze gone now, the flashback disintegrating.

"Think about it, Rob," David urged. "You just said

I left you in Nam. I ran out on *you*, not Cory Rugby. You—Rob Thornton. Doesn't that tell you something?"

Rob scowled. "No, nothing. You're just trying to confuse me."

"No, Rob, I'm not. I'm trying to help you."

"Help me? How?"

"Isn't Cory Rugby dead?" David pressed gently.

Rob sank back on the piano bench and shook his head ponderously. "I don't know, Dave. I honestly don't know."

CHAPTER
EIGHTEEN

It was Saturday morning, a crisp hazy day with scudding, mottled, wind-tossed clouds hugging the horizon. We had been up for hours preparing for the Vietnam Veterans Memorial Service in Riverside. David, Lance Edwards, and Commander Thomas had all arrived in time for one of Eva's delectable cheese omelets. I noted that there was a special, private camaraderie between Eva and the Commander today. He was jovial, attentive, and generous with his compliments. "Eva, my dear, I wish I could sign you up in the Navy. You could teach our chefs a thing or two."

Even Lance Edwards seemed unusually mellow. He and David lingered over their coffee long after Pam and I had cleared the table. Rob, still in his bathrobe, had barely touched his breakfast. Agitated and distracted, he had excused himself early to go shower and dress. I wasn't sure whether he had been uncomfortable in the presence of Commander Thomas or simply nervous over the approaching ceremony. I still wondered whether he would allow himself to be introduced during the service, especially as a war hero.

Shortly before it was time to leave, Pam asked, "Where's Rob? If he doesn't hurry, we'll be late."

"We're all going in separate cars," I told her, "so why don't you and Lance go on and save us some seats?"

Lance snickered mildy. "With so many driving, I figured we were forming our own little caravan to escort our hero in proper style."

Commander Thomas silenced Lance with a sharp, withering glance.

"I make no claims to being a hero," Rob said from the doorway.

As we all turned, Eva gave a startled gasp—a mixture of shock and pleasure. Rob stood ramrod straight, strikingly handsome in full dress whites, his Navy headgear tucked crisply under his arm, his Lieutenant insignia on his shoulder epaulets. Most astonishing of all was Rob's face. He had shaved his beard. His clean, chiseled features accented his deep azure-blue eyes, giving him a fresh, boyish vulnerability, an appealing charm.

"Man, do you look gorgeous!" exclaimed Pam. She went over and gave him an impulsive kiss on the cheek.

"Oh, Rob," cried Eva, "you look just like you did the day you left for Vietnam. You've seen the picture, Michelle. Doesn't he look just the same?"

"He sure does," I agreed.

David's voice was gravelly. "You look just like I remember, Rob. It takes me back quite a few years. Almost makes me wish I was in uniform again."

"Sure gets the attention," said Rob, sounding

pleased, flattered. He looked around, nodding at the Commander. "I guess we'd better go, sir, before I change my mind."

As it turned out, we did form a caravan of sorts, Commander Thomas and Eva leading the way, Pam and Lance riding behind them, and David's Mercedes bringing up the rear. Rob and I rode with David at the end of the procession—but not for long. David was not one to linger in the slow lane. With a quick wave of his hand, he passed the others and sped along the Riverside Freeway, turning off at the Van Buren exit. After several miles, as we approached the March Air Force Base, we turned right into the Riverside National Cemetery. The sight of an endless row of American flags—swirling Stars and Stripes flapping in the April wind—stirred a profound sense of patriotism within me. Immediately David and Rob fell into a hushed silence, as if snapping to attention. We followed the curve of the road until we spotted the sprawling Plexiglas replica of the Vietnam Veterans Memorial. We parked and joined the several hundred people gathered around the somber, gleaming black wall, scanning and examining, touching and tracing the infinite rows of names.

Eva came over and stood beside Rob. She clasped his arm, steadying herself and dabbing her tears as she stared up at the imposing, sun-washed panels. "Imagine all the grieving parents who so lovingly selected these names for their children."

The Commander slipped his arm comfortingly around Eva's waist. "I checked the log book and found the location of your son's name." He led us over to the middle panel. "Here it is—Robert A. Thornton, Jr."

Eva lovingly traced the name, moving her fingertips gently over the small white block letters. Rob stood beside her as if frozen in time, his face like granite, motionless except for the pulsating tendon along his jawbone.

I leaned over beside him and gazed at his name, then scanned the ones around it. Glancing over at the Commander, I said, "Most of the names have a tiny diamond in front of them; a few have crosses. Do those symbols mean something?"

"The diamonds indicate those who were killed in action and the crosses are for the MIA's," explained Commander Thomas.

"But there's a circle around the diamond beside Rob's name," I pointed out.

The Commander's usual stoic expression grew suddenly tender as he clasped Rob's shoulder. "Rob represents the only man on the entire wall who has returned alive. If by God's miracle more of our men are found alive someday, there will be more circles."

Eva stepped back and surveyed the entire wall. "These rows of names—they have a life of their own," she murmured. "It's as if I can feel their spirits parading into my heart or hear their voices in the wind. It's as if they've been allowed to come home at last and be honored for the heroes they are." Tears coursed down her cheeks. "I know how every mother's heart grieves and yet beats with pride when she touches her son's name on this wall. No matter how many memories fade, the names remain alive." She looked at Rob. "Oh, my son, I am so fortunate to have you back. If only all these other mothers. . ."

We lapsed into silence for several minutes, allowing the wall to work its mesmeric, magnetic effect on us, those silent names speaking with a collective, spell-binding transcendence.

Finally, David patted my arm. "We'd better take our seats, Michelle. The ceremony is about to start."

"Oh, but wait. I forgot my camera. It's in the car."

David retrieved his keys from his pocket. "Go ahead and sit down. I'll be right back."

Rob stepped forward. "Let me go, Dave," he said, his voice cracking slightly. "I need a minute alone."

"Sure, buddy." David tossed Rob the keys.

By the time Rob returned with the camera, the U.S. Air Force Band was just beginning the National Anthem. Rob stood tall, unblinking, his rich baritone blending with the crescendoing instruments. The anthem set a regal, reverential tone for the entire ceremony, from the presentation of the Colors by the Marine Corps Color Guard to the solemn presentation of the wreaths and the dramatic twenty-one gun salute.

As a National Gold Star Mother delivered the main address, I glanced around at the crowd. A stern, square-jawed Marine sat nearby, unmoving, his eyes riveted on the wall. Veterans in camouflage fatigues or combat jackets and faded jeans stood off to one side in subdued clusters. Families sat huddled together; toddlers played quietly at their mothers' knees; elderly couples held hands. Many people brushed at unbidden tears.

Following the main address, the master of ceremonies stood and introduced Commander Thomas. I looked over quickly at Eva. She gave me a knowing smile.

Commander Thomas seemed to have no question about his part in the program. He marched swiftly up to the podium. Looking out across the sea of teary, breeze-swept faces, he said in his splendid, booming voice, "We have come here today to honor our heroes on the wall. Our patriots listed here paid the highest price freedom can cost. They gave their very lives. Some etched here remain among the missing, but we proclaim the same message to them as the MIA/POW flag so boldly declares: 'You are not forgotten!'

"This powerful wall stands as a solemn yet sublime interface between us and our lost patriots," continued the Commander, "reminding us that we are each held accountable for the freedoms we take for granted every day." He pointed to the center panel. "The Memorial's inscription reads: 'IN HONOR OF THE MEN AND WOMEN OF THE ARMED FORCES OF THE UNITED STATES WHO SERVED IN THE VIETNAM WAR. THE NAMES OF THOSE WHO GAVE THEIR LIVES AND OF THOSE WHO REMAIN MISSING ARE INSCRIBED IN THE ORDER THEY WERE TAKEN FROM US.' "

The Commander's gaze moved over the audience and settled on Rob. A smile flickered on his lips. "Ladies and gentlemen, we have a rare opportunity today to welcome home and to our hearts the only veteran listed on this wall who has come back to us after all these years. Lt. Robert A. Thornton, Jr., would you please come forward? We would like to honor you in a special way today."

Rob shrank back momentarily. I thought for sure he would bolt and run. I reached over and squeezed his hand supportively. With slow, inevitable motions, he rose and made his way toward the podium. My heart sang with a mixture of pride and sympathy for Rob. This was perhaps the most glorious and terrifying moment he had known in years.

If only he would accept the praises and the accolade of the crowd rather than consider such profuse attention a threat to his carefully guarded privacy.

Commander Thomas's voice rose over the roar of the Air Force jets soaring overhead as he said, "Lt. Thornton, over a decade ago after your shootdown, when you were presumed dead, the President of the United States awarded you posthumously the Congressional Medal of Honor, our nation's highest award for bravery, and presented it to your mother. It gives me great honor on behalf of your mother and our country that you so faithfully served, to personally present this medal to you."

The Commander draped the medal around Rob's neck, then stepped back and saluted. After returning the salute, Rob gripped the lectern with one hand and leaned on his cane with the other. He cleared his throat nervously. "In a very real way I represent the heroes on this wall. I—I really don't deserve it, but I'm accepting this Medal of Honor for those 58,000 men and women on the wall who should be here to receive it."

As Rob turned from the rostrum, there was a burst of applause from the audience. The square-jawed Marine nearby was the first on his feet. Then quickly the entire crowd rose in a standing ovation.

I wept. Eva cried softly. Even David had tears in his eyes.

When the ceremony was over, Rob, visibly shaken, said, "I want to see Cory's name."

Lance left Pam's side and approached Rob. "You say you want to see Cory Rugby's name? It's right over here. He was one of the last to go down." Lance led us to the center panel and underlined Cory's name with one long finger. I glanced at Lance's expression. He looked as if his face was about to shatter, as if he were engulfed in a private grief of his own. Could he possibly have felt this same intensity of emotion with every MIA story he had followed, stricken as though it were his own personal loss?

Rob moved over where Lance had stood, knelt on one knee beside the glistening panel, and removed his headgear. He pressed his palm flat against Cory's name and bowed his head against the facade. Wrenching sobs gripped him. "Oh, God, oh, God, oh, God!"

A hush fell over the milling throng around us as Rob continued to weep bitterly. Finally, David drew me aside and whispered, "We're going on over to the Veterans' Reception across from the cemetery. You and Rob come over when he's ready."

I kissed David's cheek. "Thanks for being so understanding. Rob needs this time at the wall, and I think I should stay with him."

David managed a tight smile. "Yes, I think he needs you. . .for now."

Eva leaned down and embraced Rob briefly, then stood and walked on with David and the others. For a long time Rob remained kneeling, his head pressed against the black, gleaming panel. His sobs had subsided now, but his shoulders still heaved convulsively as he drew in gulping breaths.

At last he stirred, as if rousing from some great inner emotional conflagration. His face was blanched, his eyes wide and tear-rimmed. There was something in his expression I'd never seen before. He could have been someone else, a stranger.

I linked arms with Rob and gave him my best smile. "I'm so proud of you. When you spoke, it was from your heart. Beautiful!"

Rob was too distraught to answer. We forged a path of our own away from the curious crowd, across the neatly trimmed lawn, up a sloping hillside to a row of marble-white monuments. We sat down beside a slender grave marker and faced the back of the Vietnam Memorial.

Streams of Old Glory were still rippling in the breeze. The vivid reds, whites, and blues formed a striking contrast to the hazy pastel pinks and oranges of the mid-afternoon sky.

I looked closely at Rob. "Are you okay? Would it help to talk?"

He stared at the ground. "I—I don't know where to begin—"

"I'm listening."

Rob's sturdy jaw clenched and relaxed. "For a moment, Michelle, as I stood on that podium and watched the flags, all sorts of memories flooded back. I remembered the Vulture, the North Vietnamese guard, shoving that picture in my face of a Communist flag flying over the Capitol in Washington. I am so grateful that never happened." His eyes grew intense as he looked at me. "I'll tell you one thing, Michelle, those years in the prison camps taught me something about priorities. God, country, family. I'm going to get it all sorted out yet."

He reached out and caressed my face, his voice assuming a fresh tenderness. "Do you know how much you mean to me, Michelle? How much I need you?"

"I know that's what you think, Rob," I stammered. "I'm glad we're friends. I'm glad I've been able to help you. . ."

"I'm not talking about being friends," he countered. His strong, chiseled face seemed suddenly fragile. "I love you, Michelle."

"No, Rob, you only think—"

"I want you to marry me."

I pulled back, stunned. "Marry you? I—I can't marry you, Rob. I—"

It was as if I had slapped him. "Why not, Michelle? You broke up with Dave because of me."

"You don't understand—it's not the way you think." I stumbled over my own words, trying desperately not to crush him. Not now. Not here where he had just been honored. "Dear, dear Rob," I faltered, "I'm very fond of you—"

"Then say it, Michelle. Say you love me."

"Rob, no. I can't."

"Why not? Your engagement with Dave is off. There's nothing stopping us now."

"Oh, Rob," I cried, "don't you see? There never was a choice. I've always loved David."

"But you and I—"

"You and I are friends, Rob, good friends. But it can never be anything more."

Pain split across Rob's face, twisting it. "But I love you, Michelle. I need you." He took the car keys from his pocket—David's keys to the Mercedes. He dangled them on his finger, eyeing them curiously. The jingling noise struck at the icy silence between us.

As if hypnotized, Rob held up the keys and shook them, making the jangly sound again. "It's like the turnkey," he said vacantly. "I dreaded that sound for years."

"Turnkey?" I repeated. "What do you mean?"

Rob's eyes glazed over. His voice grew hollow, his

words almost rote. "Back in the prison cell—when the guards came—when we heard those keys turn in the rusty, worn latch, we knew we were facing another siege of unrelenting interrogation. And more humiliating... excruciating... torture."

"I know how terrible it must have been for you, Rob."

"No, you don't know, Michelle. You haven't the faintest idea. No one can ever know who hasn't been there."

I held out my hand tentatively. "Rob, I'll take the keys for you. We probably should get over to the reception."

"I'm not going, Michelle." He pocketed the keys. "I've had enough of people ogling me today. I don't want to be with anyone except you."

"Rob, please—"

"It's true, Michelle. You're all I have now. Without you I have nothing to live for."

"You don't know what you're saying."

Rob's entire frame shuddered. His face turned livid. "I know exactly what I'm saying! If you won't marry me, Michelle, I might as well be dead!"

I reached out urgently for him, but he was already on his feet, glaring down at me. "You're just like all the rest—running out on me. I'll show you, Liana—uh, Michelle. No one will ever run out on me again!"

He wheeled around and took great, long, limping strides across the cemetery grounds toward the road—and David's Mercedes!

"Wait, Rob!" I shouted. Panic clutched me as I realized he planned to take David's car. He hadn't driven—shouldn't drive. Not in his frame of mind. The desperation and hysteria building in Rob could lead to only one thing: suicide!

I threw off my heels, grabbed them, and ran after Rob. I reached the automobile just as he slipped into the driver's seat. He started the engine. I dashed around the front of the car to the passenger side, swung open the door and leaped inside just as Rob peeled away from the curb. He torn down Van Buren at breakneck speed, heading for the freeway. Scaling the onramp, he swerved right toward San Bernardino.

"Rob, please, be reasonable," I begged. "Pull over and let me drive."

"I'm driving," he growled. His hands shook violently on the wheel.

My own fingers trembled as I fastened my seatbelt. "You've got to calm down, Rob. You don't even know where you're going. Home is in the other direction.

He drove on in dogged silence.

I knew from the road signs that we were heading toward Eva's chalet at Lake Arrowhead. Was Rob risking such a drive with the gathering storm clouds hovering over the mountains? His hands grew taut on the steering wheel, yet even in his fury he seemed exhilarated, power hungry with driving again. He barely braked when he turned onto Waterman, the tires screeching, squealing as he hit the gas pedal and sped on.

"Rob, slow down. You'll get us both killed!"

"You didn't have to come," he said evenly. "It was your choice."

"You needed me."

"Wrong. I just need to be free."

We had started up the gently sloping elevation toward the winding mountain curves ahead. Rob skimmed past the oncoming traffic, oblivious to the sudden rolling mist settling on us like a veil, slowly engulfing us. David's long-forgotten warning thundered in my consciousness: "If a fog cover comes in, turn around and run." Was this what David had meant—this rapid, swirling, blinding curtain blocking our view of the canyon and valley below, impairing our visibility of the road ahead?

Rob was creeping along now, his fingers moving frantically along the dashboard for the right controls. Our headlights cast a faint beam through the fog; the windshield wipers took their dry swishing journey across the clouded pane. It didn't help.

"Turn around and go back, Rob. You can't even see to drive."

"Where do you suggest we turn, Michelle? It's a straight drop-off beyond the guard rail." He squinted. "And right now I can't even see the rail."

Nor could we see the jagged rocky cliff jutting up on our left or the oncoming trucks until they rumbled by us. I strained to read the road signs. The Crestline turnoff. The 3000 foot elevation. Then 4000 feet. Would Rob dare risk a U-turn on this narrow, zigzagging road? The car in front of us dipped and rose with the mountain curves, then disappeared from view. Rob accelerated into the vaporous mist until the dim lights of the car ahead reappeared.

My hands were clammy, my mouth parched from sheer terror. "Rob, please—"

"We can't go back, Michelle. There's no way."

"Then find a way," I begged, "before you ruin David's car." I regretted my words at once. Rob's jaw tightened. My mind reeled. Did he intend to plunge us over the shadowy precipice?

"If I crash this Mercedes, Michelle, we both go

with it."

"Is that what you really want, Rob?"

"I thought I did, but . . . I don't know. How much farther is it to Eva's cabin?"

"We just passed the 5000 foot elevation. But it's foolish to keep climbing in this fog."

"It would be worse to pull off the road. The next car might not see us. We'll wait it out at Eva's."

My thoughts raced. Would David and the others even think about looking for us at Lake Arrowhead? Or would they go home to Irvine expecting us to be there?

More importantly, would Rob and I even reach Eva's? If Rim Forest was still on the map, we had missed it. And I was certain that we had passed the turnoff to Blue Jay Village as well. The minutes ticked away. Silent ones. I kept praying, "God, give me strength. Don't let me fail Rob now. Keep me calm."

Finally Rob veered left across the scant roadway, nearly colliding with a huge, phantomlike truck that emerged from the mist. For another thirty minutes we inched along the Two Mile Road, winding, twisting, snailing along over the fog-shrouded mountain paths to Eva's isolated chalet tucked in the conifer forests surrounding Lake Arrowhead.

Rob had no trouble remembering that Eva hid her extra key under the woodbox behind the house. He unlocked the back door, and we entered the chill, faintly musty cottage. He dropped his Navy headgear and keys on the table, then opened the curtains. I stealthily scooped up the keys and slipped them into my pocket as Rob walked to the living room and put a log on the fireplace. I shivered as he struck a match and ignited the dry wood.

"Sit down, Michelle," he said, stepping back from the flames. "Relax."

"We can't stay here, Rob. We should go home as soon as the fog lifts."

"You have time to rest," he said quietly, pulling me down gently on the rustic sofa beside him. "It's peaceful here with just the two of us. No one can intrude. We have all the time in the world, Michelle."

"No, Rob. David will be worried. And Eva—"

He touched my hair lightly. "Forget David, Michelle. Forget everyone else—"

I moved away nervously and reached for my purse on the massive oak coffee table. "I just remembered, Rob. I have something to show you. It came in the mail last Wednesday. I intended to tell you about it the other day, but Lance arrived."

"Tell me what, Michelle?"

"About the clippings. I've done some sleuthing on my own and I've found Cory Rugby's hometown."

Rob sat forward, startled. "Cory Rugby?"

"Yes, I've learned some fascinating things. You were right when you said he came from a military family. His father's a retired Army Colonel." I paused, watching Rob's reaction.

"A Colonel?"

I fished in my purse for the envelope from Winterset. "And Cory had a brother, Rob, a younger brother—"

"A draft dodger," finished Rob with a scowl.

"How did you know that?"

"I don't know. It's just there in my mind."

"Do you remember anything else about Cory?"

"I. . .I mean, he. . .I don't know, Michelle."

I handed him the clipping with the photographs

of the Rugby boys. "Perhaps this will help, Rob."

He stared at the pictures. His hand began to tremble as he pointed at Cory's photo. "I've seen him before, Michelle. I do know him!"

"Who is he, Rob?" I urged.

"It's me—Cory." He shook his head as if to clear it. "No, not me—my friend." He stood abruptly, grabbed his cane, and paced the floor. "It's there, Michelle, it's there. Why can't I reach it?"

"Try, Rob." My excitement was mounting. "Was Cory your friend in Vietnam?"

"My friend? Heaven help me, Michelle, if he was my friend—" Rob stalked the room wildly now, running his cane over the roughhewn stones of the fireplace, clutching the photo in his free hand. He was talking to himself with a strange desperation, his words clipped, erupting in staccato phrases, his face alive with agitation. "Come on, Cory, we'll make it—not much farther—we've got to make it—!"

"Rob, what is it? What's happening?"

He looked my way, not at me but at some distant point in space, his eyes fine black pinpoints—that familiar, dazed, agonized expression that struck terror in my heart. Clearly Rob was back in Vietnam, reliving some shattering, nightmarish event.

He stared up at the antique cavalry saber above the fireplace. "It's all right, Cory. They won't take us alive!" He reached up for the gleaming sword, his cane rattling to the floor. Waving the blade, he rushed blindly past me, limping out the front door, crouching down, carrying the saber poised ready to strike at an unseen enemy. "I'll kill anyone who tries to stop me now!" he shrieked. He stumbled down the porch steps and lumbered toward the towering, mist-cloaked pines.

I sprinted after him, shouting, "Rob, come back! Stop!"

He plunged on, no longer aware of me, his Navy uniform creating a pale, ghostly apparition as he wove among the trees in the dusky twilight. I heard him scream out, "Go on, Cory! The border's just ahead. You can make it! Don't come back! It's too late for me!"

He hid behind one tree, then another, chasing shadows, darting in and out, propelling himself forward, as if by sheer grit he would outstrip the wind.

Long, unbearable minutes passed as I pursued Rob through the murky woods. At last I caught up with him. He was swaying now, reeling, dragging his injured leg. "No, Cory, no!" he pleaded. "Why didn't you listen to me?..." Suddenly, without warning, he pitched forward and crumpled to the ground like a wounded man, his saber tumbling freely beside him. He crawled on his belly, painstakingly inching his way along for several feet through the lush ferns and scrubby thicket. Exhausted, he lay on his face panting and weeping.

Then, with a fresh burst of energy, Rob pushed himself to his knees. With his bare hands he began digging vigorously, deliriously in the thick moss and moist earth. "Why did you do it, Cory?" he demanded. "You didn't have to die! My friend, my friend, you were almost home free. Why did you do it, Cory? Why did you die for me?"

CHAPTER
NINETEEN

I knelt down beside Rob as he pounded the un-yielding sod, entreating his unseen, long-dead comrade to forgive him.

"Rob, you're not in Vietnam," I said, slipping my arm around him. "The war is over. You're home. You're free."

He grew still. His hands relaxed on the scarred earth. He raised his head and gazed at me, his eyes intent, imploring. "Free?"

I felt as if I were watching his very soul emerge from dusky, delphian depths. He sat back and looked around at the rugged, spiraling pines, their upper branches lost in the remnant wisps and puffs of lingering fog. "It happened a long time ago, didn't it?" he asked.

"What, Rob? What happened?"

"Cory died. My friend, Cory Rugby. I saw it, Michelle."

"Tell me, Rob."

He drew in a deep shuddering breath. "I remember

now—Cory and I were making our escape from the North Vietnamese prison camp. After a week of hiding by day and traveling by night through the jungle, we were only a few yards from the Laotian border and freedom. We could hear the patrol running hard after us, their sandals slapping a thundering beat on the trail. Cory had already scaled the final hill. I was falling behind, limping badly, my old leg wound grossly infected. I caught my foot in a gnarled root and stumbled."

"Oh, Rob—"

Tears welled in Rob's eyes and rolled down his dirt-streaked cheeks. "Michelle, Cory—my good buddy Cory—turned around and came back. I begged him to go on without me. He wouldn't listen. He just kept coming toward me. He was smiling. I can still hear him calling, 'God helping us, Rob, we're going to freedom together!' "

Rob wiped his tears on his uniform sleeve. "Cory never even saw the soldiers. They riddled him with bullets. His smile froze on his face as he collapsed. The blasted patrol didn't even know I was there, cowering a dozen feet away. Michelle, I couldn't move, couldn't say a word, couldn't raise a hand in Cory's defense."

I reached out and brushed Rob's hair gently back from his face. "I'm so sorry, Rob. So very sorry."

"It was my fault, Michelle. Cory died because of me. He shouldn't have come back for me. After he was shot, I just lay there, too terrified to go to him. I was scared the soldiers would find me too. Shoot me. Or worse. Take me back to the prison camp.

"Hours later, just before dawn, I crawled on my belly to Cory. My brave friend, who for eight years never once gave up hope that he would go home, was gone, dead." Rob's tears were unbridled now. His words came in quick, short gasps. "With my bare hands, I dug a shallow grave and buried Cory. I saluted him and whispered 'The Lord's Prayer.' Then I staggered wildly, insanely over that last hill in broad daylight into Laos, not knowing that country, too, had fallen to the Communists. But no matter what happened, I had to keep my promise to Cory."

"What promise, Rob?"

"In the prison camp, after the missionary Dick Evans died, Cory and I made a survival pact. We memorized each other's home phone number. We promised that if anything happened to either of us, the other would get out somehow and call his buddy's family and tell them how he died, tell them he loved them." He looked up with sudden comprehension. "Michelle, the numbers I kept writing—"

"Yes, Rob. They were Cory's home phone number."

"Then that's still a promise I have to keep." His gaze lowered solemnly. "What will his parents say when I tell them Cory died because of me? It's as if I killed him, Michelle."

I pressed Rob's head against my chest. "No, Rob, it wasn't your fault. You didn't kill Cory. You've carried the guilt all these years needlessly."

"But—"

"No, Rob. Look at me. Listen to me. Your friend came back to help you. Wouldn't you have done the same for him?"

Rob's eyes riveted on me, so intense, so poignant. "We would have di—" The word hung unfinished between us.

"Were you going to say you would have died for each other?"

Rob nodded, a look of peace passing fleetingly over his face. A chill easterly wind whistled through the fir trees. I reached over and took his hand. "It's getting dark, Rob." I said as I stood up and urged him to his feet. "The fog is lifting. We need to go back down the mountain. We need to go home."

We brushed the pine needles and moss from our clothes as we walked back to the house. Once inside, I called Irvine, but Eva's line was busy. Rob was surprisingly calm as he bent and spread the dying embers in the fireplace. We found some canned food in the kitchen cupboard, fixed a quick snack, tried reaching Eva again—without success—then locked the doors and started down the porch steps to the car. At the foot of the stairs, Rob broke off three red buds from the rose bush by the trellis. "For Mom," he said quietly.

The low swirling mists had blown clear; the moon and stars were beginning to sprinkle fragile shards of light across the evening sky as we pulled away from Eva's chalet.

"Thanks, Michelle," Rob said as we drove down the mountain toward Irvine.

"For what?"

"For standing with me, believing in me. For helping me find Cory Rugby." He paused meaningfully. "And Rob Thornton."

I kept my eyes on the narrow, winding road. "It's what I've prayed for, Rob."

Tentatively he asked, "Do you think I'm crazy, Michelle?"

I glanced over momentarily. "I know you're not,

Rob. You've had a long journey back from hell itself. You've survived."

"Survived maybe. But is that enough?"

"It's a beginning, Rob. You've unlocked the past and faced your darkest secret—that haunting fear of having killed someone. Now you know the truth. You're not to blame. You've taken the first step back to being really well. Don't let go now. Not when you're almost home."

I felt his hand caress the back of my neck. "I still love you, Michelle."

I drew in a careful breath. "Rob, you're just beginning to be free to love—really love. Someday the time will be right and someone very special will come into your life."

He removed his hand, but I could still feel his eyes on me. "There was someone special once..."

"I know, Rob. Liana."

"Liana?"

"Yes, Rob. Do you know how many times you've called me by her name—even today at the Memorial?"

"But she left me, ran away." He spoke from wrenching pain. "I can still feel her tears falling on my face when she said goodbye."

"If she was crying, then she didn't want to leave you, Rob."

"Then why did she go?"

"When you first came home, the Commander told us you had been very ill with cerebral malaria. He said a young Hmong woman and her companions brought you safely across the swollen Mekong River, during the monsoon rains, to the refugee camp in Thailand. She risked her life for you, Rob. She must have loved you very much."

"I loved her too," he said yearningly.

I phrased my words carefully. "Do I remind you of her, Rob?"

He was silent a moment. "Yes, Michelle, I guess you do. You don't really look alike, but you have the same shining, flowing hair, the same graceful walk and caring manner. Your voice is soft and gentle like hers—"

"So, Rob, perhaps all this time you've simply loved Liana through me."

Rob's voice grew troubled. "If Liana smuggled me across the Mekong River, she may never have made her way home again. The Mekong is always treacherous, not just during the monsoons. It's patrolled constantly by makeshift gunboats. It's the illegal, forbidden bridge to Thailand—and freedom. Few people make it across, and never by day. Few have the courage even to try anymore."

"Perhaps Liana's still in the refugee camp in Thailand," I said.

"Waiting for me?" he wondered aloud.

"And if she were?"

"I don't know, Michelle. For four years she was my whole life. But now? So much has happened. I need time to think it through."

"You have time, Rob. And people who care. We'll all be there for you."

"I'm just beginning to appreciate that fact, Michelle."

We lapsed into an amiable, exhausted silence for the rest of the trip home. It was after eleven when Rob and I arrived back at the condominium. Lance Edwards' car and the Commander's were parked just behind Eva's. All the lights in the house were on. Even before Rob and I reached the porch, the front door opened and David came striding out.

"Michelle, are you all right?" he cried, taking me in his arms. "We were worried sick. Where in the name of heaven have you been?"

"It's my fault, Dave," said Rob quickly. "I was upset. I took your car. I'm sorry."

David glanced from Rob to me, puzzled. "As long as you're both okay—"

"Better than okay, Dave," Rob acknowledged. "I *remember*."

Before David could respond, Eva and Pam scurried out toward us. Pam embraced me as Eva lifted her arms to Rob. "Oh, my son, thank God you're all right."

Rob swept Eva up in a hearty embrace. "I'm home Mom, really home!" he declared.

Eva drew back in tears. "Rob, are you saying—?"

"I remember everything, Mom. I know I'm your son. I remember the last time I saw you before going off to Nam." With a flourish he presented her with the three rose buds. "These are for you, Mom. I gave you roses when I went away and roses now that I've truly come home." He bent down and kissed her cheek. "I love you, Mom. Will you forgive me for hurting you?"

"Yes, my darling, a thousand times over." Eva clasped the roses to her breast and wept without restraint.

"Let's go inside," suggested David, his voice husky with emotion, "before we all catch cold."

Lance and Commander Thomas stood in the doorway, wary concern written on their faces. They stepped back as we entered, everyone talking at once, excitement snapping in the air like electricity.

Amid the anxious questions and confusion, Rob

held up his hands in a quieting gesture. "Please, everyone sit down. I have something to say."

A pronounced silence gripped the room as we settled quickly on the sofa or in easy chairs. My stomach knotted with tension. For an instant the pictures on the wall were larger than life; the drapes swayed; the floor spun. All the struggles and suffering we had been through these past four months—the feuding and suspicions, the questions and secrets—would be revealed now and finally put to rest.

An expression of pain ingrained itself in Rob's lean face. He cleared his throat, then said in an almost inaudible voice, "I need to tell you what happened in Southeast Asia."

"You don't have to, son," Eva said, resting her hand on his. "You've been through too much already."

"Yes, I do, Mom. We need to talk about it once and for all. And then go on with living."

Lance scowled from across the room, waiting. He was sitting on the arm of the chair beside Pam, his face as ashen as Eva's. He kept his eyes steadily on Rob. "Go on," he challenged. "I want to know about your time in Indochina whether your mother does or not."

"I need to go back quite a few years," said Rob, appraising Lance with a passing scrutiny. "Back to that last flight with you, Dave. Back to the grenade explosion. When the hulk of our plane blew, I was hurled into the underbrush. I vaguely remember hearing you call my name. I attempted to answer, but my voice was muffled by the crackling fire and the multiple explosions that followed."

David's knuckles whitened as he gripped the arm

of the sofa. "That's incredible, Rob. You called me and I never heard you. I was sure you were dead."

"I was—almost. The leg I injured when our Phantom crashed was open and bleeding. My gut ached and blood oozed from my mouth. Eventually I slipped into unconsciousness." Rob ran his fingers distractedly through his hair. "When I came to, North Vietnamese soldiers were poking me with the butt of their rifles, laughing triumphantly as they dragged me over the muddy trails to the prison camp. Even then, I tried to find you, Dave. I really did. I tapped out messages all through that prison. Whenever there was another shootdown, I'd ask the new guy if he had seen you. Finally, Dave—" Rob's voice cracked. "—I decided you were dead."

David's hand found mine. His eyes were wet, glistening. He choked out the words, "Oh, Rob, all these years we've both thought the other was dead. If only we'd known—"

Rob sat forward on the love seat beside Eva. "We'll make up for lost time, Dave. That's a promise."

"You've got a deal," said David. He took out his handkerchief and blotted his eyes.

"Where does Cory Rugby fit into all this?" quizzed Lance.

"I'm getting to that," said Rob. "It was months into my captivity before I met Cory. And then some time after that, we became friends with the missionary, Dick Evans—a big, gentle-hearted guy who just wanted people to know God. He never meant the Vietnamese any harm.

"There were others, too," Rob went on. "Some guys sold their souls for a crust of bread or a cigarette. But most of us hung on somehow. It wasn't easy. Every one of us spilled our guts at one time or another. Wrote confessions. Made up names and locations for troops and ships and those in command. It didn't seem to matter to the North Vietnamese what we said, as long as we weakened."

Rob stared across the room at Commander Thomas. "We tried to live up to the Code of Conduct—'resist by all means, keep faith with your fellow prisoners....' Oh, God, how we tried, but..."

The Commander's usually stoic face seemed somehow malleable, moving subtly with finite emotional impulses. "Let's get this straight, Lt. Thornton," he thundered, "every POW broke at least once. The Rambos and John Waynes never made it home."

For several long moments Rob stared somberly at his hands. His voice was splintered now. "As the months dragged into years, we were certain the war had ended. The guards told us America had lost, been defeated by the Communists. We wondered if we would ever get out, ever taste freedom again. That's when Dick, Cory, and I made up our minds to escape. It was after our second attempt that our interrogators separated the three of us from the others and sent us to a slave labor camp. They called it 'reeducation,' " Rob scoffed.

"Pure brainwashing," remarked David.

"At least we were together in the 'reeducation camp,' and freer to talk. In spite of his recurring malaria attacks, Dick Evans would pray and preach sermons and fight his own spiritual battles before us. When the guards took away his torn, threadbare New Testament, he still sang, still told Cory and me that God was in control. Cory grabbed on to the idea at last and found his measure of peace and joy in Christ. I was scornful in the beginning; then for want of something to keep my mind alert, I started memorizing Scripture verses: the Beatitudes, Psalm 23. At first they were rote, but over the years those verses dug deep into my soul."

"Forget the missionary," demanded Lance. "What about Cory?"

"I'm getting to Cory," Rob answered quietly. "In our sixth year of captivity, Cory and I buried Dick Evans. From then on Cory assumed responsibility for our spiritual needs. I'd play my imaginary piano, and we'd sing the hymns Dick had taught us. Cory added 'The Old Rugged Cross' and 'We're Marching to Zion' from his Sunday school days in Winterset."

I glanced over at Lance. He was hungrily taking in every word Rob said.

"Cory never gave up hope—the belief that one day we would be free. 'Our country won't let us down,' he kept telling me. 'If we're the only men left here, they'll find us.' "

"We tried to find you," Lance said in a raw whisper. "I followed every lead in Thailand, Vietnam, Laos, everywhere. They were all dead ends."

Pam patted Lance's knee. "Don't feel bad, Lance. You did more than the rest of us."

"Tell me, Rob," Lance urged, "did Cory make it to Laos?"

Rob's eyes darkened in desolation. "He tried. One day while we were working the rice paddies in the north, I told Cory, 'We're only a few days' journey from Laos. We've got to make a run for it.'

"They might kill us," he argued.

"I'd already dropped forty or fifty pounds," continued Rob. "I was flesh stretching over bone. We didn't have mirrors, but we could look at each other and see how bad we looked. 'They'll kill us,'

Cory repeated. Then he threw back his head and laughed ironically. 'I'm with you, Rob,' he told me. 'We haven't got a thing to lose but our lives.' Then he looked at me so peaceful-like and said, 'Don't you remember what Dick used to tell us? *Absent from the body. Present with the Lord.* They can only kill this poor flesh. Inside,' he said, thumping his hollow chest, 'there's a new man. A man ready to meet Christ. You've got the same opportunity, Rob.' "

"Oh, Rob, Cory was so right," said Eva.

Lance interrupted. "And did you try to escape?"

"The next day," replied Rob. "We eluded capture for a whole week, traveling by night over ill-defined trails, wading across narrow streams and rivers, navigating by the stars—always keeping close to cover, ready to dive into the bamboo thicket. We passed a downed B-52, an abandoned American truck, and rusting helicopters lying wasted like scrap metal. We collected water off banana leaves and ate moths and berries. We were just in sight of the Laotian border..." Rob's voice broke. He leaned forward and buried his face in his hands.

It was evident he couldn't go on. Quietly I said, "While they were running, Rob tripped and fell. He told Cory to go on alone, but Cory came back for him. He wanted them to see freedom together. Tragically, Cory was ambushed before he reached Rob."

Lance hung his head and slowly massaged his temple, averting his eyes so that I couldn't read his expression.

Rob still wasn't ready to speak, so I haltingly continued the account. "Rob buried Cory in a shallow grave that he dug with his own hands. He's blamed himself for Cory's death all these years. The shock of Cory dying for him, followed by Rob's malaria, must have triggered his amnesia."

"I'm no doctor, but I imagine it's all part of the post-traumatic stress syndrome," offered the Commander. "With survivor's guilt mixed in."

"I went to pieces after that," Rob said, his voice edged with contempt. "Cory's God—Dick's God—where was He? I didn't want to face life alone, but I made it to Laos because I wanted to keep my promise to Cory. I traveled alone for days, side-stepping Laotian soldiers and machete-wielding hill people, hiding in a cave as black and cold as the coal bin from my childhood, drinking water from a mosquito-infested stream. I knew I was getting sick—tremors, violent headaches, nausea—but I kept going. Feverish with cerebral malaria, I dreamed of my friend Cory Rugby. Apparently I called his name during my delirium. When I awakened in the Hmong village, a young woman named Liana was taking care of me. She called me *Cory Rugby*. In my stupor I thought, *Cory Rugby? I must be Cory Rugby. I am Cory Rugby.*

"After that I forgot days and years. I was caught in a time warp. I slipped naturally into the culture of the Hmong people, accepted them as my own family just as they accepted me. I could remember nothing from my past, not even my promise to Cory."

"What promise?" Eva asked.

Rob shifted to face Eva. "Mom, I told Cory that if I made it back home, I'd call his parents and tell them what happened to him...and tell them he loved them."

Without warning, Lance jumped to his feet and asked imploringly, "And my brother—did my brother have a message for me?"

Every eye turned his way. Eva uttered an astonished gasp that echoed through the hushed room. Rob and I glanced comprehendingly at each other, then back at Lance.

"You're Cory's kid brother!" Rob declared. "That's why I felt as if I knew you. Your eyes, your profile—the way you cock your head and square your shoulders—you do look like Cory."

"How can it be?" I protested incredulously, staring Lance down. "You're Lance *Edwards*!"

He looked almost contrite. "Edward was my middle name," he explained. "I had my last name changed because I couldn't live up to the Rugby reputation."

"Then you're from Winterset?" I pressed. "You're Colonel Rugby's other son?"

"Not that he'd admit it, but yes, I'm Lance Rugby."

"So that's why you traveled all over the world tracking down MIA's," I charged. "You were looking for your brother."

"That's about it," said Lance. "I was in Thailand when I heard the rumor that an MIA claiming to be Cory Rugby had been found. But my hopes were dashed when he was identified as Rob Thornton. I beat it back to the States to track Thornton down. I knew there had to be a connection between him and my brother. Otherwise, why would he think he was Cory?"

I studied Lance, then framed my question carefully. "From the beginning you were convinced that Rob had harmed your brother. Isn't that why you stalked him so relentlessly?"

A faint smile played on Lance's lips. "Exactly, Michelle. Rob claimed amnesia. He acted guilty.

What else was I to think?"

"It's what I thought too," Rob admitted. "But now I know—Michelle made me see—Cory's death wasn't my fault."

Lance shifted restlessly in his chair. "I wish—"

"What, Lance?" coaxed Pam.

"I just wish I could absolve my own guilt so easily."

"Your guilt?" I pressed.

Lance twisted his college ring with a sullen edginess. "You already know I took the easy way out, Michelle—ran to Canada like a yellow-bellied coward while my big brother went off to fight my war for me. My father never forgave either of us—Cory for disappearing in Vietnam without a trace or me for running out and tarnishing the lofty Rugby military tradition." He sighed heavily. "But what hurt most was my brother's disappointment in me for not wearing a uniform and defending our country. He never forgave me."

"But he did," Rob insisted excitedly. He stood and approached Lance. "Part of my promise to Cory was to find his kid brother and tell him he was forgiven. Cory loved you, man. He wanted you to know."

Lance gripped Rob's hand, released it, then stumbled over to the window and wept brokenly. "Maybe I've finally bought my peace at home," he reasoned at last. "I'll go back to Winterset and tell my parents that Cory is dead—that he died a hero—that he made his peace with God. If I can share these things with them, maybe they'll have room in their lives for me again."

Commander Thomas stood, his manner brisk and efficient. "Eva, I need to use your phone. Do you mind? I must get the wheels in motion—notify the

Navy that Captain Rugby won't be coming home."

"Sir," Rob offered, "perhaps Lance and I could fly to Winterset together. I want Cory's parents to hear from me personally how bravely their son died."

"Rob, dear," said Eva with quiet pride, "going to Winterset is an excellent idea—the proper thing to do."

Pam sprang up and clapped her approval. "Hey, this evening's turning out all right after all! Let's celebrate. Anyone for a pizza?"

"Count me in," Rob declared.

David was standing now too, smiling, pulling me up beside him. He tilted my chin and kissed the tip of my nose. "Everyone else is picking up the pieces, Michelle," he whispered. "How about it? Do you think we could pick up where we left off?"

I flashed my most alluring smile. "That's the nicest invitation I've had all evening."

"It's just the beginning, my darling," he said in his low, provocative voice. He glanced over at Rob. "But first a little unfinished business."

Blinking back happy tears, I watched as David turned to Rob, reached out unashamedly, and gave him an enormous bear hug.

"Friends again, Rob?" he asked.

Rob was all boyish grin. "Sure, Dave. Friends forever!"

CHAPTER TWENTY

During the next six weeks, David and I spent many long hours together slowly, cautiously rebuilding our relationship. We talked through our personal and mutual goals, our expectations, our private hopes and dreams. With love and patience we reached a new plateau of respect and understanding. David was happier and more relaxed than I'd ever seen him. Even Eva noticed the change.

For that matter, all of us were in high spirits now that Rob was making such dramatic strides toward his recovery. With his discharge from the Navy imminent, I was free to return to work full-time at Ballard Computer Design. Best of all, David and I were able to see each other every day, often spending leisurely lunch hours at cozy restaurants or picnicking in a nearby park. Usually we were too enraptured with each other to eat, so we fed our sandwiches to the ducks and swans.

On the third Monday of May, shortly after David and I had returned from our lunch break, Mitzi Piltz scurried over to me and whispered confidentially, "Have you noticed how peculiar Mr. Ballard has been acting lately?"

"Whatever do you mean, Mitzi?" I asked, stifling a smile.

She spoke in a high, breathy voice. "Well, he walks around with the strangest little grin on his face and laughs to himself when nothing is funny. He was in his office all morning with the door shut, and whenever I knocked, he said he was busy. Yet I heard him whistling and humming to himself, so I know he couldn't have been working."

"Maybe he's just in a good mood," I suggested lightly.

"Well, maybe so, but he's been very mysterious, too. Usually he asks me to put through his phone calls, but today he's been making them all himself. You'd think he was planning some sort of clandestine activity, he's been so secretive lately."

"I'm sure Mr. Ballard has nothing to hide, Mitzi. He's a very proper, circumspect man."

Mitzi gave me a narrow, scrutinizing glance and mewed, "Yes, I suppose you would know that, wouldn't you?"

David arrived in time to save me from a biting retort. "Michelle, got a minute?" he asked.

I thought of saying *I've got a lifetime*, but Mitzi was craning her neck like a hungry vulture, hanging on every word. I was relieved when David ushered me into his office.

"I've made plans for Friday," he announced.

"Friday?" I echoed, mildly baiting him.

"Yes, Friday. It's your birthday, isn't it? Your 25th?"

"You remembered," I said, pleased.

"How could I forget? You circled it on my desk calendar."

"I did not! You circled it." I eyed him curiously. "What plans did you make?"

"I thought we'd take Friday off. Get an early start. Have a pleasant little evening out. Who knows? Maybe we'll wing it."

"Fancy or casual?"

His eyes twinkled. "Why don't you wear that dusty rose evening gown with the sequin trim and chiffon cape?"

"That's the fanciest thing I own."

"Exactly. Who knows where the evening will take us?"

David wasn't speaking idly when he mentioned winging it on Friday night. He arrived wearing his Pierre Cardin tuxedo with the powder-blue cummerbund, escorted me promptly to his Mercedes, and drove north toward the Los Angeles International Airport. As we drove under the sign, LAX DEPARTING FLIGHTS, I asked, "David, are we having dinner at the airport—dressed like this?"

"We're meeting an incoming flight."

"Whatever for?"

"Could be someone important on board," he said evasively.

"One of your clients?"

"Not exactly."

"Oh, David, not our friends Jackie and Steve Turman!"

"No, it's a TWA flight from Chicago, not Morro Bay."

"Don't tell me Joshua Kendrick is coming to see us."

"Our friend with the DEA? Don't think so." David

was grinning slyly as he pulled into the twenty-four hour parking lot. He parked and ushered me out of the car with a sweeping gesture. "Come, lovely lady." He tucked my hand into his and piloted me into the crowded airport past curious onlookers toward the security check. We made a funny, carefree, frolicking pair—David disarmingly handsome in his tux, a camera case swinging at his side, and me in my dusty rose gown, trying not to trip as we cantered through the corridors, my heels clattering on the polished walkway.

"David, they won't let us through without tickets."

"I've got tickets on the four o'clock flight to San Francisco."

The shrewd, tight-lipped security guard frowned as he took the camera case from David. His brows arched as he examined the contents. He snapped the case shut, winking conspiratorially, and said, "Get some good shots, sir, and you, miss, have a good evening."

"David, why are we going so far for dinner?" I asked as we boarded the plane. "I'm already starved!"

"San Francisco has the best prawns on the West Coast."

"Be serious, David."

"I am, Michelle. Fresh prawns—they melt in your mouth." He gave me a merry glance. "You do like prawns?"

"You know I do."

He reached over and fastened my seatbelt. "You'll love San Francisco—there's a spectacular view at night."

"David, what if I freeze to death in this flimsy cape?"

"Then I'll buy you a fur coat to go home in. Or better yet, I'll just keep my arms around you."

When we arrived in San Francisco an hour later, a sleek, white limousine was waiting for us. The stocky, boyish-faced driver bowed slightly from the waist. "Happy birthday, Miss Merrill. I'm John, your chauffeur for the evening."

The sight of him made me giddy. He looked uncomfortable, his chubby self squeezed into a tuxedo with a pink-salmon cummerbund, his unruly black hair slightly mussed, his toothpick caught in one corner of his mouth.

John sped us along the streets of San Francisco, in and out of the traffic, toward the waterfront, finally pulling to a stop in front of the luxurious Hyatt-Regency at the Embarcadero Center. John whipped around the limousine, opened the door, and helped me out. "See you at 9:30, sir," he told David.

"What are we doing in this hotel, David?" I asked uneasily as he whisked me through the plush, carpeted lobby to the elevator.

"Trust me, Michelle. We're just going to eat."

Moments later we stepped into the Equinox, the circular, revolving restaurant at the top of the Regency, high above the gusty city. The maitre d' promptly led us to a candlelit table for two by the window where we had a panoramic view. "Have a pleasant evening and a happy birthday, Miss Merrill," he said as he seated me.

"David, does all of San Francisco know it's my birthday?"

"I'd rather all of San Francisco know that I love you." He reached across the table for my hand as

a young woman with sparkling eyes and a whimsical smile stopped beside our table, set up her music
stand, opened her violin case and, seconds later,
began to play, "I Left My Heart In San Francisco."

The attractive violinist continued to serenade us
with a selection of romantic ballads and classical
numbers as the head waiter prepared our dinner
at our table. He tossed a Caesar Salad, adding spices
and freshly diced carrots, cucumbers, and celery
with a flourish. The plump, brown prawns sizzled
over the open flame beside a wok of crisp, stir-fried
vegetables. We watched the waiter spoon out
steaming bowls of cream soup with melted strands
of mozzarella cheese. As he placed them before us,
he said suavely, "The entire restaurant is enjoying
your music."

"Our music, David? You arranged this?"

"Just for you—with a little help from the Music
Consortium of San Francisco."

We ate leisurely to the golden, lilting strains of
Mantovani, surrounded by a galaxy of orbiting city
lights below us.

"I'm a lucky man, Michelle," David said after
dinner. "I think these past few weeks have been
good for us. You know, for awhile I thought Rob
would never forgive me for loving you. But now that
he's found himself, he tells me he's glad you and
I are together again."

"Rob told you that? He really is a miracle. God's
miracle."

"And so are we," David said softly. "I just hope
someday Rob finds someone as wonderful as you."

"I want him to be happy. Since he and Lance came
back from visiting the Rugbys in Winterset, Rob's
been more at peace with himself."

"And with God?"

"Eva's sure it won't be long, now that his heart is growing tender toward God." I paused meaningfully. "Besides, he's already reached another important decision."

"What's that?"

"Rob's determined to find Liana. He won't rest until he finds her and knows she's safe. Eva's with him one-hundred percent."

David nodded. "I think Liana's the one he's loved all along."

"So much has happened lately," I mused. "Eva has packed away all of Rob's old memorabilia. She's fixing his room up the way he wants it. They're both ready to close the file on the past."

David's gaze lingered on me. "And I'm ready to open the file on the future—a new beginning for you and me."

My heart skipped a beat. Was David finally going to—?

My thoughts scattered as the waiter arrived with dessert. He balanced a small sterling tray on his palm with two matching silver goblets on a lace doily. His eyes twinkled, and his mustache wiggled as he placed them on the table before us. "This one's for the birthday lady," he intoned.

David waited quietly as I opened my frosty goblet. My spoon froze in mid-air. Inside was a dainty open jewel box with an immense solitaire diamond glittering in the flickering candlelight.

"Happy Birthday, darling." David's voice was rich and tender, his dark eyes alive with love. "Michelle, I love you, cherish you. Will you marry me?"

I wasn't sure whether to laugh or cry. My whisper rose like a shout in the hushed room. "Yes,

David, yes. I'll marry you."

David took the ring and slipped it on my finger as the violinist guided her bow smoothly over the mellow strings. Leaning across the table, the candlelight glowing on his face, David tilted my chin and kissed me with a slow, tender passion. A sudden burst of applause from the surrounding diners broke our romantic reverie.

Later, when we left the restaurant, John was waiting with the limousine. "Well, sir," he said as we settled into the velvety, cushioned backseat, "did she?"

David held my hand up triumphantly. "She did!"

"Then let's celebrate," said John. "I'll find you one of the best views in all of San Francisco." John whisked us around the steep, twisting streets, meandering up one narrow avenue and down another, zigzagging crazily at last along the crooked maze of Lombard Street. We followed the cable car downtown to Fisherman's Wharf and made our way across the Golden Gate Bridge, stopping finally at the picturesque Vista Point Lookout. John squinted at us through his rearview mirror. "You've got a few extra minutes, sir, before you have to catch your midnight flight home."

David and I left the limousine and strolled over to the high, windswept bluff overlooking the Pacific. I shivered as the chill ocean breezes swirled around us, whipping my tawny hair against my cheeks. David opened his jacket and, in a sweeping, cloaklike motion, enfolded me against his chest. His solid warmth enveloped me like a cocoon.

"Would you consider eloping, Michelle," he ventured, "or do you still want that summer wedding?"

I gazed up at his strong, angular face, his handsome features silhouetted by the moonlight. "David, I've dreamed of the flowers and frills of a garden wedding since I was a little girl."

He kissed my forehead, my lashes, my lips, then whispered in my ear, "A garden wedding then, my darling."

For what seemed an eternity we stood nestled together, spellbound by our love, our dreams entwined and wafting into a night as crystal-clear and star-studded as the diamond glimmering on my finger.

MES